Return to the Pack

Rejected Mate

Book Three

Alexa B. James

&

Calinda B.

For my loyal readers.

Alexa B. James & Calinda B.

Chapter One

Luna

The Jacksonville pack's Alpha might be dead. The latest in an endless string of hurricanes is blowing through the city with relentless fury, taking Axel's home to the ground with him inside.

With a scream, I throw down the sandbag I'd been carrying and race toward the debris.

The wind catches a piece of the siding and whirls it toward me like a deadly guillotine.

"Look out," Callan cries, launching himself at me. We crash to the ground, barely escaping having our heads chopped off by the sharp metal edges of the siding.

We sink under the cold, churning water around us, only to be yanked back up by Warrick. I inhale a lungful of air as my head leaves the water.

"Let me go," I shout as the wind blows my words into the air. "We've got to save Axel!"

"I just saved your life, baby girl," Warrick growls. "I'm not going to lose you now."

"Thank you," I call over my shoulder as I dive toward the rubble of the fallen house.

From what I can make out in the gloom of night, Ethan and Callan are already pitching aside lumber, broken windows, dishes, and other things that once occupied Axel's house.

Each of their flashlight beams provides weak light in the blackout that just plunged Jacksonville into a hellish nightmare. All around me, gusts of wind hurl the remnants of other houses through the air.

I expect to see humans, cars, and people's pets flying through the air at any moment.

My three lovers charge forward, holding their flashlights between their teeth as they work, frantically trying to find Axel in the floating debris.

I join my triplet lovers, working side by side with them. We tear apart the piles of what was once a perfect home but is now nothing but an unrecognizable jumble of housing material.

My mouth isn't big enough to get a good grip on the flashlight, and it falls into the wreckage a minute later. "Shit," I cry, giving up on finding it and screaming for my last mate instead. "Axel! Axel!"

Ethan looks up at me, his face owl-bright in the glow of the flashlight, pausing in his quest to find Axel.

"He could be drowning in there," I cry, waving my arms frantically.

Return to the Pack

Ethan sets to his task with more fervor, tearing away the bits, leaning into the wind, and searching for Axel.

We all pitch in with renewed vigor. Axel might be alive, and we'll all risk our lives to find him if he is.

This is *so* not fair. After warring with one another in animosity, we finally made peace and agreed to work together as a family. And Warrick agreed to be Axel's Second in Command. We'd just begun getting along when the storm hit, and now it's all been ripped away.

I toss aside a piece of siding when I touch something clammy and soft. *Is it...? Could it be?*

"Y'all," I yell. "I think I found him!"

The triplets surge in my direction and help me uncover the rest of him. We work quietly but swiftly until Axel's entire body is revealed.

I step back a second, unable to face what might be my biggest heartbreak of all. I spent most of the last few months hating Axel and then loving him but pushing him away. We only reconciled tonight, and now...

"Is he... Is he dead?" I whisper.

Warrick crouches, gets his arms underneath Axel, and lifts him from the water and into the pounding rain. "Check him out, brother."

Callan places his fingertips on Axel's carotid artery. "I got a pulse," he says with a grim nod. "It's faint, but it's there. Let's get him out of here."

My knees buckle, and I practically fall to the ground I'm so relieved.

Ethan places his hands on my shoulders to steady me. "Easy, girl. Let's go."

We make our way to what once was the front of the house. Luckily, the little rowboat we used to trek to the pack member's home in our rescue effort is still affixed to what's left of the porch railing.

Warrick gently lays Axel in the boat, and we all push through the horrible storm. "We've got to get out of the city," Warrick yells over the wind. "Our place is on higher ground and less likely to be flooded. We'll go there to take shelter and see to Axel's injuries. No way can we drive from *here*—the water's too deep."

"And then what?" I shout back. We can't carry Axel while in wolf form, not when he's out cold.

Warrick grins. "We hotwire a human's abandoned vehicle and drive it home. I got no problem with that. Any of y'all?"

"Nope," we all say in unison.

If there's anything that Warrick holds dear, it's trouble and lawlessness.

I hold Axel's hand while we slog up the street. It's cold but when I grip his wrist, I can sense a faint pulse.

Making our way out is grim business. Houses everywhere are destroyed. The city's really taking a beating.

Return to the Pack

The wind continues to rage and howl. If I weren't so worried about Axel, I'd be scared for all of our lives.

After about a twenty-minute walk, moving as quickly as we can with the force of the wind pushing at us, we get to a place where the water is only up to our ankles.

"Let's take this truck," Warrick shouts.

I feel a little funny about that because Mama always taught me that we couldn't take from others to help ourselves. But the house is flattened, which means the occupants have either left or they're dead, so I nod along with the others.

Warrick and Ethan head to the tiny truck and fiddle around inside the cab. A few minutes later, the engine roars to life.

"Axel needs to be in the cab where it's warm," I call. "I'll sit next to whoever's driving, and then you can rest his head in my lap. Of course, he'll have to be scrunched up, but at least he'll be warmish."

"You drive," Warrick says to Callan. "It's a one-seater, and I barely fit. We might need weight in the back if this little pickup has rear-wheel drive, anyway. I'll ride in the bed with Ethan."

Callan gets behind the wheel, and I slide in next to him.

Warrick maneuvers Axel's limp form into the seat, with his head on my thigh. He reaches for something behind the seat and retrieves an oily, grimy blanket which he drapes over Axel's body.

Axel looks so pale that I want to cry. I run my fingertip across his cool skin.

Please live, Axel. Please, please, please, *live.*

Once the other brothers are situated in the bed of the truck, Callan pulls the truck away from the collapsed house. The truck rocks back and forth with the wind. The tires spray water on the side of the truck even when we go slow, getting Ethan and Warrick more drenched than they're getting from the downpour.

When Callan has inched his way out of town, he presses on the gas pedal, and the speed picks up a little. The windshield wipers are on full tilt, but the rain obscures our vision as fast as the wipers clear it.

"Fuck," he mutters, peering through the wall of water.

Axel groans.

"Axel!" I run my palm over his cheek as his eyelids flutter open.

He gives me a blank-eyed stare, and then his eyes close down again.

"Axel, my love," I say. "My Alpha. Are you with us?"

Axel says nothing. His skin now looks a ghostly yellowish-white.

"He's probably in shock, Luna," Callan offers. "The best thing we can do for him is to keep him as warm as possible."

Although I don't really know what shock is, it sounds serious. So I lapse into silence for the duration of the terrifying ride to the boys' home.

When we arrive at their dwelling, I'm relieved to see it intact. The storm rages, but the trees offer some protection from the gale force.

Before Callan even has the truck parked, Warrick and Ethan leap out of the truck bed.

Warrick opens the passenger door and extends his hand to me. I take it and slide my rump from the seat.

He wraps his arms around me for a brief but tender embrace. His skin feels chilled to the bone, and he's a sopping mess, but the hug is more welcome than he'll ever know.

When he releases me, I step to the side so he can retrieve Axel.

"Callan, support his head and shoulders and scoot him toward me," he orders. "I don't want to just yank him out."

"Good call," Callan says. "We don't know the extent of his injuries. Be as gentle as you can but move as quick as you can, too. There's a golden hour to meet for medical trauma, and we're well past that. His life hangs in the fates' hands."

They move as swiftly as they can with their precious cargo, and before long, Axel is in Warrick's arms.

Warrick hurries through the rain to the house, where Ethan stands holding the screen door.

"Put him in my room," Callan says, glancing at me.

When I lived there, he gave me his room. Now, he's giving it to Axel, our Alpha.

I stay beside Warrick, who steps over the empty beer cans and fast food wrappers cluttering the floor. Looks like since I moved to town, the boys are back to their old swamp dog ways. Warrick lays Axel on the unmade, messy bed like he's a porcelain doll who might shatter.

Right now, nothing matters except his well-being. I huddle next to Axel, clueless as to what to do next. Callan hustles into the room with his medical bag. He snaps his fingers and points at Ethan. "Get rubbing alcohol and bottled water, stat."

"On it," Ethan says, hustling out of the room.

"Can you get a blanket, Luna? This boy's skin is near ice."

"You got it," I say, grabbing the blankets from the floor next to the bed.

Callan retrieves a set of weirdly curved scissors and starts cutting Axel's pant leg from the ankle.

"What are you doing?" I say.

"We strip 'em, then we flip 'em. We don't got time to gently peel Axel out of his clothes. We already lost way too much time getting here." He makes the last snip at the waistband. "You peel the clothes away as gently as you can while I keep snipping."

I nod, thankful for more to do than watch. I pry back Axel's jeans to see a swollen bulge, mid-thigh, along with extensive bruising.

"Shit," Callan says, glancing at Axel's leg.

"What?" I say, alarm cinching down on my heart.

"Looks like a nasty break. Okay, done with this side. Keep going." He moves alongside Axel's body until he can get to his sopping shirt.

Ethan returns with the supplies Callan requested and lays them on the bed.

I gently tug the wet clothes away from Axel's skin. His other ankle bears a similar swelling as his opposite leg. More bruises mar every square inch of his legs.

Callan kneels beside Axel and palpates his body.

Ethan uncaps bottles and hands them to Callan as requested. Warrick tears from the room to gather ordered supplies from Callan's sharp instructions.

Callan tucks the blanket around Axel's torso as he gets to work splinting his leg and ankles.

The room blurs all around me as whispers fill my head.

Luna...

9

I frown, glancing around to see where the whispers are coming from.

Everyone is focused on Axel.

Luna…

What? I move my lips silently, mouthing the word.

Luna…

I think Axel's the one saying my name.

As activity continues all around me, I fell into a semi-trance.

Axel's got a hold on me, more potent than our previous True Mate ritual bond.

The ferocity of the bond scares me. And yet, it draws me like a moth to a flame. I seem bound to follow it, even if I burn to a crisp in the fire.

Chapter Two

Luna

It takes a few days of constant care to keep Axel from falling over the edge into the unknown world of death to join Mama. I don't think I could take losing another person I love. Luckily Callan's been in and out of Axel's room every few hours over the last few days, changing bandages, applying some gooey salve to Axel's scrapes and bruises.

Sometimes I clean Axel with a basin of warm water and a washcloth, lovingly caressing his ravaged body with the cloth. But for the most part, I watch over him to make sure he still breathes.

Outside, the wind still howls and constant rain drenches the land.

Callan, Ethan, Warrick, and I barely say a word to one another as day falls into night and night yields to dawn. If I eat, I don't remember eating. If I sleep, I barely track it—I'm too caught up in this strange connection I share with Axel. Nevertheless, his whispers continue to fill my head.

Don't leave me, Luna. Never leave.

I won't, Axel. That's the past.

I don't think I'm gonna make it... The void is calling to me.

No, Axel, you can't leave us! You have four wolves waiting for you and an entire pack to lead. And me...

I cuddle into him and hold him close.

Finally, at dawn after five days of rest, Axel rolls over, looks into my eyes, and smiles.

A flood of elation fills my heart. "Axel! You came back to us."

His eyes drift closed, but the smile remains. He draws a trembling stroke along my cheek and down my neck. "You didn't leave," he says in a rasp.

"No," I say, unable to think of anything clever to add. "I never will."

Axel opens his eyes once more with a groan and pushes himself up to prop his torso on the headboard. "Well, fuck... That hurt." He chuckles weakly. "Even laughing hurts. Did I break my ribs?"

"A few. And you broke your femur and your tibia. I learned those words from Callan." I beam proudly at my Alpha, and he nods, looking as proud as I feel.

"You'll be a regular medic with him around."

"You okay?" I ask, squeezing his hand.

"When the house came down all around me, I thought I was a goner, that's for sure." His eyelids drift closed again.

"Can I get you anything? Water? A beer?"

"'A beer,' she says… What a good nurse you are." Axel chuckles again. Then, opening his eyes, he directs them at me. "I am hungry, in fact. Thirsty too. Can you fetch me some food and water?"

"Anything," I say, eager to serve my Alpha. I hurry out to the kitchen where Warrick sits, smoking.

"Good news," I say.

"It must be if you're smiling. Haven't seen much of that pretty smile of yours lately."

"Now I got something to smile about," I say, unable to keep the grin from my face.

The corners of Warrick's lips curve upward. "Tell me the good news," he says, tapping the ash from his cigarette into a chipped white bowl. He takes one last pull on the cigarette.

"Axel's awake!" I grin like I just discovered Mama's risen from the dead. It ain't Mama, but it's the same to have someone else I love come back from the brink.

"Is he now?" Warrick stubs out his smoke and gets to his feet. "We'll have to check in with my medic-minded brother, but you probably shouldn't give him too much food. He hasn't eaten for days."

"But he's a wolf," I say this triumphantly, like being a wolf conquers all.

"Right," Warrick says, striding toward the fridge. "And wolves, like anyone, can yak up a quickly consumed

13

meal after days of hunger." He opens the door and peers inside. "We got some duck stew here. Maybe a bowl of that to start."

"Where are Callan and Ethan?" I glance into the front room. "I want to tell them, too."

"They'll be back shortly. They just took the bikes out for a ride. They were getting in my hair. It was more of a demand than a request." Warrick chuckles in his deep, throaty voice—it's more of a gravelly growl.

The wind batters against the back of the house, rattling the screen door against its hinges.

"When do you think this blasted storm will end?"

Warrick glances toward the back door. "It's bound to ease up soon, maybe today. Already dying down."

The sound of roaring motorcycles fills the air.

"I'll check with the boys and see how things are looking in Jacksonville." Warrick hands me the duck stew. "Dish him up some stew. If he finishes it, tell him to wait a bit before wolfing down more."

"Got it." I nod and reach for a bowl in the cupboard. I use it to scoop some savory soup, licking the dribbles off the side of the bowl. I grab a spoon and head back to the bedroom.

Axel's sitting at the edge of the bed. "How long have I been out?"

"A few days," I say with a shrug. "How you feeling?"

"Good as can be expected, which isn't great. But I'm alive." He flashes me a wan smile.

I hand him the duck soup and the spoon.

He lays back on the bed, as if he's too exhausted ot even sit. I slide onto the bed next to him, taking the bowl into my lap. I take a spoonful and lift it carefully to his lips. He hesitates, like he's unsure if he can give me that kind of rule of him. But then he opens his lips, letting me feed him like a baby. My heart hammers in my chest with each bite. I feel powerful and needed and wonderfully loved as I feed him, as if it's what I was always meant to do.

We don't speak a word the whole time, but something weighty fills the air, a charge that makes my pulse scamper like a swamp rabbit.

Right as he finishes, Callan, Ethan, and Warrick tromp into the room, interrupting whatever was happening. I quickly busy myself with licking out the bowl.

"Axel," Callan says, medical bag in tow. "Looks like you made it out of the woods."

"I seem to have," he says. "Thanks to y'all." A warm smile curves his lips, and he directs his attention at each of us in turn.

"We didn't have anything better to do," Ethan says gruffly. "This damn storm has kept us all cooped up in here."

"Happy to provide some distraction," Axel says with a wry smile. Slowly, like an ancient man, he rises.

Callan retrieves his stethoscope from his medic bag. "Easy, man. You've been more or less in a coma for the last few days."

"Yeah," Axel says, sort of sit-falling onto the bed. "I'm a little dizzy."

"You probably need water. So get Axel a bottle of water, Ethan," Callan says.

Oh, dear. I forgot the water. I chew on my lower lip.

Axel seems to sense my guilt. "That stew was damn delicious. Did you make it?"

I shake my head. "No. I've been by your side day and night."

He holds out his arm, and I just about dive into it, so grateful to be curled against his side. After kissing the top of my head, he says, "Thanks, y'all. Truly. I'm grateful to still be alive."

"Of course," Warrick grunts. "If I tried to take over the pack, they'd tear me limb from limb. They don't even know I'm your Second. Although... That could be fun." He cracks his knuckles and grins.

"Oh, they know, I can guarantee that," Axel says. "Pack bond. News travels fast, even in a storm. Speaking of storms...." He turns his attention to the window, which for once isn't being hammered by rain. "Has it passed?"

"One sec." Callan fastens his blood pressure cuff around Axel's arm and inflates it. Next, he affixes the stethoscope's diaphragm to Axel's inner arm and slowly lets the air out. "Blood pressure's good. Okay, now you can ask questions," he says, draping the stethoscope around his neck.

"Weather's dying down," Ethan says. "Callan and I just got back from a ride on our motorcycles. Clouds are dissipating here and toward Jacksonville. They're moving south, back where they came from."

Axel nods. "Any news come in while I was out of it?"

"Nah," Warrick says. "Nobody was leaving their houses in this."

"We should probably head into town and check it out—see who needs help," Alex says.

"With the strength of this one and the damage we saw on the way out of town, a lot of people need a lot of help," Warrick says.

Axel nods again. "Good man."

"*Great Second*, you mean," Warrick counters. "I don't take my responsibilities lightly." A somber expression falls upon his face.

"I knew you were the man for the job. Let's go." Axel tries to stand but falls back on the bed again. The mattress frame springs creak in protest.

"Easy there, Alpha," Callan says. He grabs Axel's wrist and places his fingers, feeling for his pulse. "You need to take it easy. We've worked too hard to get you to this point. You're not going anywhere until you're ready."

"I can't just lay around here. I have a pack to take care of," Axel protests.

"You *can,* and you *will* stay put. Listen to Callan. He's the expert here," Warrick says, crossing his arms over his giant chest. "You can use your pack bond to let the others know you're alive. We'll do intel on who needs what. We'll give you a full report when we return."

Axel groans but says nothing, his face pale and miserable.

"We'll leave our baby-girl here to keep you company," Warrick says, nodding toward me.

I'm as eager as anyone to get out of the house. But I smile gamely at Warrick. "Sure thing, Daddy. I'd love to keep Axel company."

"Before you go, I'd like to make a request," Axel says, assuming his Alpha dominance. It shines in his eyes and the tilt of his head.

"What is it, Alpha?" Warrick says, fully locked into his role as Second.

"Y'all really stepped up to the plate and came out swinging. I couldn't be more impressed or proud to have you as a part of the pack." Axel nods at each man.

Callan, Ethan, and Warrick all stand tall, their pride evident.

"You, too, Luna," Axel says. "As soon as possible, I'd like to swear you all into the Jacksonville pack in an official ceremony. We'll stand before the others and declare you, Warrick, as my Second, and you two, Callan and Ethan, as pack members. If the other pack members see you working on their behalf for the next few days or weeks—whatever it takes to start the process of repairing the damage and getting everyone housed—they'll be happy to embrace you." His jaw is set in a way I've grown to admire.

This is why he's Alpha—he wears leadership like he wears his own wolf skin. It's as natural to him to lead as it is to breathe.

The brothers nod.

"As for you, Luna…." He holds out his hand to me.

I take it, savoring the warmth coming from him, ecstatic that he's alive. Electrical sparks shoot between our hands, reminding me of the special connection we share.

"I'd like you to join the council of decision-makers," Axel says solemnly, still working even if he can't physically return to his role just yet. "You'd be an excellent addition to the pack. You've got fresh ideas, a level head, and you're one of the fiercest, most loyal wolves I know."

I consider his request as all eyes are trained on me. Looking out the window, I stare at the trees still bending and swaying in the wind. Finally, I turn back to Axel and say, "Thank you for your offer. But I must respectfully decline."

Axel's shoulders sag slightly.

I squeeze his hand. "I'm honored you'd even consider me, and I could try it if it's what you order. I'll obey my Alpha and my Daddy Warrick. But if you're giving me a choice to do what I want... I want peace in our own home. Y'all can work on making peace with the pack or the vampires or whatnot. I want to help us all work together as a team."

"We are a team," Callan says, sinking onto the bed beside me. "You saw that during the hurricane."

"I know." Words lodge in my throat as I think of my dead mother and all I've been through in a short amount of time. "But in truth, I'm not interested in any kind of leadership positions. I was a lone wolf until recently, and I'm still getting used to having y'all around. I'm not ready for the pack to look to me. I don't think it's ever going to interest me."

"She *is* a submissive," Warrick reminds Axel, who still looks doubtful. To him, titles and positions of power are an honor, but that's because he's a dominant. I have no interest in any of that.

I extend my hand to Ethan. He takes it and lifts it to his lips, kissing my knuckles.

"Let's continue to work on peace at home," I say. "I'm sure there will be enough challenges ahead to keep us all busy, inside and out of our family."

In my gut, I sense the truth of my words.

This is only the beginning of what's to come.

Return to the Pack

When the triplets are gone, I lie down beside Axel and throw my leg over him. "How are you feeling?" I ask again. "Are you still hurting?"

"My wolf's taking care of whatever's left of my injury," he says, his hands circling my waist in a possessive hold. "How's my little mate?"

"Worried," I say, toying with the front of his shirt. "I thought I'd lost you."

"Was that a bad thing?" he asks quietly.

"Of course," I cry, squirming to get closer. It's not close enough, so I climb on top of him, laying my small body over his long one. "I still feel our bond. I was in agony all week thinking we wouldn't have more time together."

"Me, too," he says, squeezing me closer.

I part my legs when I feel his cock stiffening under me. "Do you have enough strength for this?" I whisper against his scratchy chin.

"I always have the strength to fuck you," he growls in response.

I pull up the front of my skirt, a garment Ethan bought me. Now that I know the joys of what he calls "easy access," I may never wear anything else.

Axel's big hands palm the backs of my thighs, and he pushes his hips up against mine and moans low in his throat.

I reach between us to free his cock, which is now stiff and straight. Just feeling it so hot in my palm makes wetness spring to life between my legs in preparation for his entrance. I scoot up enough to position him at my opening, then sink my pussy down slowly onto his bare cock.

"Luna," he groans, his hands tightening on my hips. "You feel so good."

"I know," I say, beginning to rise and fall on top of him, reveling in the power my body has to bring this dominant Alpha to his knees. I ride him until we're both panting for breath. When I feel his knot forming, stretching me open in a way only a True Mate can, I cry out and come hard, nearly blacking out when I feel his hot seed spurting into my core over and over.

When we're done, I flop down beside him, cuddling close and glowing with happiness. My Alpha is healing, my Daddy is happy with his position in the pack, and my two other lovers are content to share me as well. With them by my side, nothing can go wrong.

Chapter Three

Luna

The city of Jacksonville is ravaged by the storm. The triplets and I spend the next few weeks trekking back and forth to the town. Axel joins us once he's well enough to do so.

Foul-smelling ankle-deep water still fills the streets, but the level has receded enough to drive Axel's truck to town. Still, we wear thigh-high waders once we step from our vehicles. We've worked our fingers to the bone, repairing roofs, boarding up windows, using sump pumps to drain basements of water, and other tedious but valuable chores. The work's been good, though, establishing the brothers and me as helpful members of the pack.

At first, we were regarded with suspicion or curiosity or both. But when the pack saw how hard we all work, they eased up on their doubts and worked side by side with us to put their homes to rights.

The water isn't too high near Axel's former house, though it's an irreparable wreck. Axel doesn't bat an eye at the wreckage. Instead, he gives more thanks for his life having been spared, then turned to me and says, "Let's check on yours."

Next, we drive by my home, which still stands but is flooded. At least there's more left than the debris that lay where Axel's house once stood.

When the heavy work slows down, Axel and Warrick keep going into town to work with the pack on details while Ethan and Callan start looking for odd jobs to pay something they have called bills. One morning, I wake to find everyone gone but Callan.

"Where's the others?" I ask, stretching and yawning as I enter the kitchen and pour myself a cup of coffee from the pot.

"Ethan got a one-man job in town, and the others are taking care of some pack business," Callan says, rinsing his plate and setting it in the rack. "Guess it's just you and me today, pet. Want to eat on the porch?"

I take a plate of food they set out for me and my coffee and head to the porch where Callan sits down to roll a smoke. It's a sultry day today, so I'm wearing short shorts and a tight lavender t-shirt to match my hair. I sit on the swing and stretch my legs into the sunshine.

Callan licks his lips as he eyes my legs, then lifts his gaze to my face. "I thought I'd go looking for herbs in the woods today. I need to stock my medicinal supply. Reckon you want to join me? Wouldn't hurt to have someone around here who knows what's what in case I ever get hurt."

The thought of trekking through the woods with Callan floods my heart with joy. Each night, by the time we get back from town, we've all been too exhausted to hunt or do anything besides collapse into bed and fall straight to sleep. My lips roll between my teeth as I study Callan, wondering if he's also thinking we might use this alone time for more than learning. "That sounds like a great idea," I say. "We've been working pretty steadily for a couple of weeks, anyway. It would be nice to have a quieter day with just the two of us."

"There's still more work to be done in town," Callan says. "But we have to take care of ourselves, too."

I hope he's feeling what I'm feeling, that we're both horny and in need of a good fuck. But I can't tell yet. I'm not as good at reading people as the triplets are, having so much less experience in my life. Mercy on the Swamp Dogs, but I hope it's me. I could use a roll with all of them after being too busy for more than a quick kiss or two for the past few weeks.

After I eat and Callan finishes his cigarette, he gets a backpack together and tells me it's time to set off. "I brought some food, water, tools for gathering specimens, even a blanket for when we need a recess from plant life."

A smirk crosses his handsome face, and a flame of desire licks between my thighs like Axel's tongue when he gets me going.

"Okay," I say, as if I'm only thinking about herbs.

Callan studies me with a playful expression. "What's going through that bright mind of yours?"

I shrug. "Plantlife. What else could I be thinking of?"

He adjusts the backpack into position with a laugh, throws his arm over my shoulders, and we proceed into the woods with sure, bare-footed steps.

As we trek through the squishy bog, stepping around swamp grass and ducking around the Tupelo trees, my soul is filled with contentment. Sure, we just endured an immense tragedy. Axel lost his house, and we almost lost Axel. But together, we made things right. Life these days is so different from the isolation in which I was raised.

Callan's eyes are trained on the ground, scanning for whatever it is he's looking for. A twinge of disappointment twists my insides that we haven't immediately gotten physical.

"There we go…." Callan points at a cluster of low-growing green-leafed plants dotted with dainty purple flowers. "Let's get some of that. That's Pennyroyal."

"Pennyroyal," I repeat. "What's it used for?"

He taps his lips. "This one's an insect repellent, antiseptic, stimulant, antispasmodic and for bowel disorders, helps with skin eruptions, and pneumonia.... And it's also used to stimulate a lady's moon cycle."

Callan stoops and plucks a few sprigs of the plant. I crouch next to him, taking a whiff of the fragrance emitted by the plant. "That smells good."

"Doesn't it? Pennyroyal is a member of the mint family." Callan smiles at me, then says, "Open up my backpack and get out a plastic bag, will you, pet?"

I do as he asks.

He fills the baggie with Pennyroyal, stands, and hands it to me. I put it back in the pack, eyeing his strong neck and shoulders. Damn, but he's sexy.

He throws his arm around me again, and we trek through the rain-soaked swamp. Once more, his eyes scan the earth instead of me.

The day isn't going like I wanted, and I start to pout.

"Oh, look," he says, sounding excited. "Here's some Shepherd's needle. Let's get some for supper."

"Have we had this before?" I ask, trying to be as interested as he is.

"Most people think it's nothing but an invasive weed, but actually, it's pretty damn tasty," he answers. "It can also be used as a pain reliever, but the kind of pain my brothers' come home with, well... We generally need something stronger than Shepherd's Needle."

Yet again, he crouches and plucks a few handfuls. I root around in his pack and retrieve a small brown bag. Once I pull it free from the knapsack, I hand it to him over his shoulder, letting my arm brush against his neck.

He turns his head back and forth, rubbing against my arm. "You feel good. I love your soft skin."

I'm instantly aroused, my knees pinching together to relieve the aching need building between them.

Callan stuffs the plant inside the sack and hands it back to me.

After placing it in his backpack, I let my hands caress his hips and tight butt. "You feel good, too."

"Sweet Jesus, Luna. I'd hoped to get a few more plants picked before getting distracted." Rising to stand, he turns and draws me to him. "It's been hard to keep my hands off of you lately. You just grow more beautiful every day." He presses his hands against the sides of my cheeks and lowers his mouth to mine.

His kiss is electric, sending tingles through my bloodstream. I shove my hand inside his shorts, pleased to feel the rigid heat throbbing into my palm.

"Oh, fuck, Luna," Callan says, withdrawing his lips from mine.

The soft snap of a branch snags our attention.

We both pause and listen.

"It's probably a deer or something," Callan says, lowering his head to kiss me again.

Return to the Pack

His mouth is sweet and soft as he nibbles my lips.

A branch snaps closer to us.

We both still and lift our noses in the air, scenting to determine who's out there.

It's a wolf, but it doesn't smell like any wolves we know.

"Shit," we say at the same time, staring at one another.

Suddenly, Callan's eyes go wide. "Run," he yells.

But his words come too late, as an enormous half-crazed wolf tears from the woods and slams into me. He drags me to the ground and seizes my neck between his sharp fangs.

Callan shifts and is on him in a heartbeat, but even Callan looks diminutive next to this beast.

Stars appear before my eyes as Callan slams into the wolf, tearing him away from me. All I can hear are the snarls of two wolves—Callan's and my enemy.

Finally, in a show of strength, Callan manages to rip the wolf's head off. I bring my hand up to my own throat, and it comes back bloody.

Callan shifts back to human, then scoops me in his arms and races toward the house.

The other wolf lies still in the bog.

"Stay with me, Luna. It's not too bad this time, you hear?" Callan chides as I bob up and down in his arms.

"I'm not going anywhere," I say weakly.

"That's right. You're not going anywhere." Callan sounds breathless as he powers us out of the woods and into the dirt driveway. He throws open the screen and races through the house to lay me on the bed in his room.

"Ever consider turning your room into the local medic clinic?" I weakly quip.

"Ha," Callan says. "At least you have your sense of humor."

He palpates my neck.

I wince.

"Thank the devil, he only nicked your carotid."

I just want to close my eyes and drift away.

Callan opens a small, rectangular plastic container from his medic kit, which he grabbed on the way in.

"I'm going to have to stitch this up, pet," Callan says, regarding me with soft eyes. "But you'll be just fine. It's just a scratch. We have this kind of thing happen all the time. It's why I'm so good at it. Lots of practice."

I nod. "I don't feel too bad."

"This'll hurt," Callan warns. "I can give you some whiskey, or we've got something a little stronger for emergencies."

I shake my head. "Just do it."

"Take the drugs, Luna," he advises, pushing my bloody hair away from my face.

"No. I want to be like you guys when it comes to pain," I say fiercely.

"Then you'll definitely want the drugs," Callan says. "Come on, pet. We all know how brave you are. You're our warrior princess."

As Callan threads his needle, I consider. My neck throbs like a bitch. "Okay, then. But just a little."

I try to smile, but it turns into more of a grimace. I take the pill Callan hands me and wash it down with the water. Then, a minute or two later, Callan gets to work.

I'm feeling all drifty and chill, and the next thing I know, I'm waking up and it's evening outside the window and I hear voices outside.

"What the fuck happened?" Axel demands.

"Another wolf attack," Callan says, their footsteps coming closer. "Big motherfucker. His irises were like black holes."

"Shit," Warrick says, stepping into the room with the others. "Fucking drugs and the beasts who use them. Sounds like the one that got her the night she came back here from Axel's."

"I'm going to speak to some elders about the wolf," Axel says. "Same as the last wolf who attacked Luna, they seem to be some mutant variety. There were a string of attacks like this when I was a kid, killed a number of our members. I'll see how they dealt with it then, and we'll do the same now."

"Maybe Ama is sending them for me from the Afterworld," I mumble, eyes closed.

"She's not that smart," Axel says, sinking onto the bed beside me. "Don't worry, sweetheart. We'll take care of this. No one hurts our mate and gets away with it."

My heart swells with warmth. He didn't say *his* mate. He said *their* mate.

Chapter Four

Luna

When I struggle to consciousness again, I'm snuggled between two warm bodies. Turning my head this way and that, I'm pleased to find Axel on one side and Callan on the other. I pat my neck. It's all bandaged. It hurts, but I know what can distract me from the hurt. I wiggle against Callan, remembering what we were about to do when we were interrupted by the attack. If anything, the denial makes me even more ready to mate than I was then. It must be from going without it for too long.

I turn on the side opposite the wound and run my hands along Callan's muscular torso.

In the dim light of dawn, he stirs and reaches for my hand, drawing it to my lips without opening his eyes.

I squirm against his hip, pushing my heat against his thigh.

"We never finished what we started, did we?" he asks, his voice low and rough with sleep.

"No, we didn't," I whisper, hoping not to awaken Axel. I gently tug my hand out of Callan's grasp and let my fingers roam. His body is warm and solid, and just touching him makes my heat throb with wetness.

I run my hand down his hard, muscular abs and over the front of his pants. His stiff cock throbs into my hand, and he groans. "I could come with a few quick strokes, Luna. Take pity on me."

"I sure don't want you to come in my hand." I push to sitting, climb on top of Callan and straddle his thighs. My sleep-tangled hair falls on his chest as I lean over to kiss his neck. My nipples spark to life as they rub against the hair on his torso.

He reaches down to grab my hips. "Damn, pet. You feel so hot."

I position my mouth over his and softly kiss his lips. His jaw—like the rest of the guys'—is lined with several days stubble. The sensation of the coarse hair against my soft skin drives me wild. I deepen the kiss, letting my tongue flicker in and out of his mouth.

He moans and sucks on my tongue.

An extra set of hands begins to caress my back and leg. Axel's awake—yum.

Panting, I grind my wetness against Callan's rigid length.

He hisses and stills my hips with his strong hands. "Easy, pet. I don't want to come before I'm even inside you. Fuck, you smell good."

"You smell that, too?" Axel murmurs. "Like candy."

Although his right leg and left ankle are bound in plaster casts, he continues to stroke his hand up and down my thigh, pulling my knee further open so I can sink down on Callan.

When I glance over at him, his free hand is working his stiff shaft while he watches me ride Callan.

The sight of his straining cock makes me want to howl. I feel like I'll never get enough of these guys. Unable to hold back, I lean over and give the head of his cock a quick suck. He groans and lifts up, pushing into my throat. His free hand tugs aside my pajama shorts, fingering my sopping pussy. He pumps a finger into me a few times while I bob up and down on his cock, licking the salty tip.

"Luna," Axel says, his voice firm.

"Mmm?" I answer around his girth.

"Sit up," he says. "I want to see how you take it from these men."

"What?" I ask, lifting my head. A string of saliva connects my mouth with his cock, and I wipe my chin and stare up at him.

"I want to see that little pink pussy stretched open and taking every inch of his cock," Axel says, his eyes hooded with lust. "I want to see how tough my sweet little mate is, if she can take a rough pounding from these outlaws."

His words have my juices sliding down my thighs and over his fingers. Callan growls and drags me forward. Axel holds me open while Callan grips his thick length and drives it deep into my juicy core.

I cry out with bliss at the delicious stretch, and Callan lets out a low growl, deep in his throat. "Fuck, Luna. Your pussy's so fucking wet today."

I slide up and down and grind my clit against his pubic bone. "You feel so good," I say, dropping my head so my hair trails along his chest.

Callan seizes a handful of my hair and draws my face down to his. He practically devours me with his lips.

I start to moan into his mouth. I'm going to come so hard I think I'll explode. Finally, I wrench my mouth away from him and dig my nails into his chest. "Callan," I cry. "Oh, Callan, I love you so much."

"Fuck her harder," Axel commands, and Callan grabs my hair and wrenches my head back, devouring my throat while his hips slam up into me from below, fucking me so hard I see stars.

"Yes," I scream, reaching for Axel. He shoves his cock into my hand, and I pump it as Callan pumps into me with crushing force until I'm forced over the edge. I scream out my wordless ecstasy, coming in color, sound, and light, pulsing all over Callan's bare cock.

He lets loose, too, and cries out my name as his liquid heat spurts into my center again and again. Hot, wet, and sticky liquid rains down over my hand and thigh as Axel lets loose with his own orgasm, a roar tearing from his lips. We're all riding an electric wave of bliss.

Aftershocks roll through all three of us for a few minutes. I'm too dazed to move. Finally, I roll off of Callan and collapse between them. I run my hands over each of their hard bodies as they massage my breasts and nuzzle my shoulders and neck. Callan finds my slick thighs and rubs our cum over my skin, first Axel's and then dipping into my pussy to gather our release and mix our scents on my skin. The fragrance makes my wolf purr with pleasure inside me, whining for more. She's already anxious for another round, but the guys both doze off.

We all slip into a drowse at last. When I wake up again, Callan is gone, and the smell of bacon taunts me, making my tummy growl.

I roll over, expecting to find Axel next to me, but he's gone, too.

The crumpled bedding smells like yummy sex, and my wolf growls to come out and play. I should feel sated, but I could go a few more rounds, so I roll off the mattress, hoping to entice someone into more play.

Clad in a short nightie and panties, I saunter into the kitchen, drawn by the smells of whatever Callan is cooking.

He stands at the stove while Axel, Warrick, and Ethan are seated around the kitchen table, wolfing down pancakes.

"Morning, sleepyhead," Warrick says, patting his large thigh.

I pad toward him and settle onto his knee. I kiss his stubble-covered cheek and breathe him in. "Hey to you, too, Daddy. How's everyone feeling this morning?"

"Apparently not as good as you three," Ethan says with a wink. Sitting across the table from me, he picks up a piece of bacon, leans over, and holds it in front of my mouth.

I take the tasty meat between my teeth, savoring the taste of crisp, salted pork.

Callan sets a plate of sourdough pancakes in front of me, and Axel scoots the syrup in my direction. I remember the sticky syrup of our cum when he rubbed it into my skin last night, and a shiver of longing runs through me.

Warrick nudges the butter toward my plate. "The real question is how are *you* feeling?" He gently fingers my wet pussy through my panties.

I slide my knife through the butter and spread it on my flapjacks. "I feel good," I say with a sigh, squirming against his hand. "Especially when you do that, Daddy."

The men all side-eye each other and shift in their seats.

"I thought we took care of your needs at dawn," Callan says, sitting beside me. He pours a healthy dollop of syrup on his pancakes and then drizzles some on mine. Then, he forks a bite of pancake and holds it before my mouth. "Not that I'm going to deny you more."

I take the bite he offers, chew, and swallow the delicious morsel. Warrick tugs my panties aside and strums a finger back and forth over my clit. I sigh and close my eyes, savoring the food and the sensation of his rough finger on my delicate, swollen flesh at once. "I'm in heaven," I sigh through the food.

"Good, baby girl," Warrick says. "We're right here with you."

"And determined to keep you safe and satisfied," Axel says, shoving his empty plate aside. He leans back in his chair, his hungry gaze fixed on me now that he's filled his other appetite.

"We'll keep her satisfied alright," Warrick growls, circling my swollen clit with his fingertip and making me squirm on his thigh.

It's so cool to witness the camaraderie and cooperation between my men.

"Yeah, about Luna's safety…." Ethan eyes me and licks his lips. "Did you find out anything about the attack yet, Axel?"

"Yeah," Axel says, reaching for a toothpick from a small, white container in the center of the table. He tucks it into the corner his mouth, his nostrils flaring as he watches me eat while Warrick torments my pussy under the table. "Not much, but a bit of info. One of the elders, a guy named Gordon who you'll meet soon enough, said he in the old days they fought off a group of wolves who mutated from feeding on human flesh. You know and I know we're not cannibals. We don't eat other humans."

"Except pussy," Ethan says with a wink at me. "I'll eat any pussy, human or otherwise."

I moan and grind against Warrick's hand as he fingers my slick folds, teasing my entrance with the tip of a finger.

"We also know the powers that come from this act," Axel says, only casting a disapproving glance Ethan's way.

"I've eaten heart," Warrick says. "I'll eat the heart of my enemy any damn day."

Axel nods. "That's part of what makes you so powerful. And a wolf who eats more than that, who regularly feasts on human flesh… It's like a steroid for a human. Pumps up a wolf to be unnaturally strong, aggressive, and oversized."

Warrick lifts his chin, clearly ready for a confrontation, but Axel seems unworried about Warrick's small acts of cannibalism. Pride for both men swells inside me, and a wave of wetness drenches Warrick's fingers. He slowly slides one inside my heated pussy while I eat. I try not to make a sound, since they're all acting like everything's normal. I close my eyes and savor the sweet pancakes as I take another huge bite, sucking the syrup from the fork.

"Do you think Ama organized the mutant wolves before she died?" I ask, ignoring Warrick's slick finger pumping into me. "Maybe she had backups in play in case the first one screwed up."

"Like I said last night, I don't think she's that smart," Axel says. "She was wily, but not a strategic planner, and these wolves aren't a pack. They're lone wolves, and she wasn't dominant enough to organize them."

"That thing was a huge-ass motherfucker," Callan says, picking up his now empty plate and licking it clean. "Thank the devil for giving me strength to take it down before it took Luna away from us. We should head back to check he's dead, though."

"We'll do it right after breakfast." Warrick drums his fingers on the table while his other hand works a second, thick finger into my opening. "But why would anyone be after our girl? Ama's gone, and no one else could wish her harm."

"I sure don't have the answer to that question." Axel tosses the toothpick on his plate. "But I hope we can suss out some more answers before one of them gets to her." He turns to face me. "No way can you go out alone, Luna. Not until we figure out who's after you and why."

His piercing blue-eyed gaze tangles with me, and I shiver as Warrick's fingers move in a slow, sensual circle inside me while I hold the gaze of our Alpha.

"Damn straight," Warrick growls. "You're to be with us at all times. No exceptions. You can't even go out in the woods to pee, got it?" Warrick slides his free arm around my middle, fiercely protective, pinning me while he thrusts his fingers into my dripping pussy with renewed vigor.

"All my freedoms are being taken away again," I say, sinking into his chest and panting out little gasps of breath with every word.

"We have to keep you safe," Axel says, nodding. "But you're not alone anymore, little mate. You're with a pack now. I'll spread the word among the other members. We'll all watch out for you. That's what happens when you're part of a pack. You're being protected, not losing freedoms."

"Thank you," I say, lolling back against Daddy Warrick's chest and rocking my hips against his hand. "You're the best men a woman could ever have. I'm so lucky."

The guys grow silent, and the only sound is the wet, sticky sound of my pussy being fingered.

Finally Ethan shoves back from the table. "For fuck's sake, spread her legs and let me feast on that sweet cunt," he says. "We can all smell what you're doing."

Warrick pushes back from the table, still holding me on his knee. He spreads my pussy lips, exposing my slick, pink inside to the other three men. Their eyes all lock on me, their nostrils flared. But it's Ethan who drops to his knees, grips my knees, and pulls them open as wide as they'll go. The others suck in a breath, and Ethan dives in, latching onto my exposed pussy, sucking greedily and thrusting his tongue into me, fucking me with his mouth until I come so hard I soak his beard and can't move a muscle afterwards.

Chapter Five

Luna

The thought of being guarded at all times by Axel and the triplets should send me packing—but strangely, it doesn't. It comforts me. I've been weirdly clingy and want them around me at all times. I don't understand why I'm feeling this way. I'm also insatiable in wanting them in my bed at night. I *need* them with a ferocity I've never experienced before.

And, oddly, I'm less inclined to go anywhere. Maybe it's because I was severely attacked twice now and almost lost my life to whoever wants me dead. Whatever the reason, when Warrick stomps through the back door, lines of stress drawing his eyebrows together, I immediately hurry toward him, abandoning my kitchen cleaning duties.

"What is it? What's wrong?" I ask.

Instantly, his features grow blank, and I know he's got something to hide.

"Where have you been?" I sidle up to him, desperate to be close to him and draw strength from him. "What is it, Daddy Warrick?"

"Why do you think something's wrong? Can't a man walk through the door with a frown on his face? I was checking on my bike. It needs a tune-up." He smiles and throws an arm around me, guiding me to the front room where Ethan, Axel, and Callan hang out. They're listening to some head-banging metal music from the last century.

They love to listen to music like this, claiming that the music created well over a century ago, possesses an edginess and fierceness not found since.

"Hey, assholes," Warrick says, removing his arm from my shoulder and turning down the volume so he can speak.

Instantly, I miss his warmth and the safety of his big body next to mine. This clinginess that's come over me feels so foreign. Maybe it's from losing Mama, and now that I have a new family, being afraid I'll lose them, too.

"I need to talk with you for a sec, Axel. Actually, all of y'all," Warrick grumbles.

"What about me?" I ask.

"You stay put, baby girl." Warrick kisses the top of my head. "This is just some guy shit I need to talk about. It's all aimed at keeping you safe." He smiles at me, and the corners of his eyes crinkle in his sun-tanned face. "We'll be right back."

The boys tromp towards the back of the house, disappearing into Warrick's room and closing the door behind them, effectively shutting me out.

I step toward their restored stereo equipment and turn the volume even lower, keeping my wolf ears pricked so I can maybe hear what they're talking about. Then I pick up a few clothes from the floor and wander into the laundry room, which is right next to Warrick's room. When we came back here after the hurricane, the place was a wreck, but Axel must have had them clean it up, because it's just regular messy now. The beer cans and bottles are kept to a minimum, anyway.

The murmur of my men's voices sounds like bees, but I can make out some of the words.

"Couldn't find the motherfucker," Warrick says. "But there's a blood trail. He didn't get far, guaranteed."

A shiver launches up my spine. *Are they talking about the wolf who attacked me? Is he still after me? Did he live?*

My hands begin to shake.

"I did see the telltale tracks of a big, ol' gator near where you said the body was located, Callan," Warrick says.

As quietly as I can, I lift the lid of the washing machine and drop the clothes into it.

"Ha!" Callan says. "Maybe Frank had himself a tasty meal."

Frank's this ginormous alligator who lives in the swamp nearby. He scares the shit out of me, but if he ate the remains of that wolf, Frank's my ally, for sure.

Return to the Pack

I reach for the laundry detergent, but once I turn on the washer, the sloshing sound drowns out their voices, and I can't hear any more.

Damn it.

I sigh and head to the kitchen, where a few plates are stacked in the sink. I've just washed the last dish and set it in the cupboard when Ethan and Callan appear.

"Where are Warrick and Axel?" I say, carefully folding the dishtowel and hanging it over the little towel bar on the inside of the cupboard.

"Heading into town to check on some pack business. It's an Alpha and his Second bonding moment." Ethan laughs.

Alarm pricks at my skin. "What are they going to do in town?" I sidle up to Ethan and stroke my palm up and down his biceps.

Ethan slides his arm around my waist and pulls me close. "Oh, they're going to speak with the pack, gather some supplies and weapons... Shit like that."

His warmth radiates into my body.

"What are you and Callan going to do?" I ask.

He and Callan exchange a wicked look.

Instantly, my core floods with heat, easing the worry I feel about two of my lovers heading into town.

"We're going to keep you company. How does that sound?" Callan steps toward my other side, and together with Ethan, they guide me toward the bedroom. "Thanks for cleaning up our shit. You don't have to do that, you know. I'm happy to do the cleaning and let you rest your little paws."

"I know," I say, practically vibrating with desire.

"How's your neck?" Callan's gaze drops to my throat.

"My wolf has healed most of it. But I'm worried about Axel and Warrick heading into town, especially if they're planning to fight a giant wolf."

"Don't you worry about us. We're all strong guys. We can take care of ourselves just fine," Callan says, his gaze sweeping my body. "And you."

"I could use the distraction," I admit in a low, throaty voice.

Ethan chuckles.

I glance down, pleased to see the bulge in his shorts. My gaze slides toward Callan, who sports a similar outline.

"Distraction is *exactly* what we had in mind," Callan says, once more exchanging a look with his brother.

Whatever unspoken thing they were communicating, it has my pussy tingling with desire as heat rushes to my core.

"Want to play a game, Luna?" Callan asks, mischief flashing in his eyes.

My brow furrows. "A game? What kind of game?"

"Let's call it 'bad wolf,'" Ethan answers.

"Bad wolf?" My brow furrowed even deeper. "What kind of game is that?"

"A fun one," Callan says. "You'll like it. And, if you *don't* like it, just say so, and we stop."

I sit down on the edge of the bed. "How do we play?"

"I'm going to be the teacher," Ethan says, rummaging around in one of the drawers in the bedroom.

"The teacher?" I say. *This game is confusing me, and we haven't even started.*

"I realize you never went to school like me and my brothers did," Callan says. "I'll play the teacher's pet."

"What does that mean?"

"The favorite one," Callan says, grinning.

I nervously pick at the bedspread. I thought we were going to fuck, not play games that I don't understand.

Ethan turns around, and he's got a pair of glasses balanced on his nose.

The effect makes me laugh. "What are you doing, Ethan?"

"Are you talking back to me again, Miss Wolf?" He's holding a ruler in his hand, and he smacks it against his palm.

"I am? I was just asking a question."

"There's that smart mouth again, Miss Wolf. Callan, would you take off Miss Wolf's clothes? I think she needs some discipline." Ethan's expression turns stern.

49

"Discipline?" I squeak.

"Bad wolf." Ethan sits on the wooden chair in the corner.

Callan steps toward me. "Get up."

"Okay." I stand.

"Come over next to me and face the wall. You're a bad wolf."

Am I a bad wolf? I shuffle toward the wall next to Ethan and stare at the plaster.

Callan removes my t-shirt and shorts in a rather perfunctory manner. He leaves on my red lacy panties, a gift from Ethan. But I'm getting more excited about the game now that I'm being undressed.

"There, Teacher," Callan says. "It's done."

"Place your hands on the wall, Miss Wolf," Ethan says.

"Okay," I say. Excitement grows inside my belly and core as I position my hands along the white-painted surface. My hair drapes over my shoulder, covering my right breast, and I feel a surge of the powerful sensation I get when they watch and want me.

"Spread your legs," Ethan commands.

I widen my stance and peer over my shoulder at my sexy biker lover, now in a pair of glasses that make him a teacher.

Ethan scoots his chair closer and draws the wooden ruler up and down my inner thighs. He hisses in a breath as I arch my back at the sensation of the smooth pine against my sensitive skin. Then, he lightly smacks my ass with the ruler.

It surprises me, and I wince.

"You've been a naughty, naughty wolf," Ethan says.

Warmth spreads across my butt cheeks as he smacks me on the other side.

The rasp of a zipper meets my ears.

Ethan's pulling his rigid erection from his shorts.

Another zipper rasps.

I glance over my shoulder.

Callan's jeans fall to the ground, and his cock bobs against his belly. "What would you like me to do now, sir?"

I'm starting to get the game—we're pretending to be someone we're not—and a swirl of heat coils up my spine.

"Stand on the other side of her," Ethan says.

Callan moves into position. "Ready, teacher."

Ethan runs the edge of the ruler along my crack. "So, talking back to me—you've been doing that a lot, Miss Wolf. I'm going to have to spank you."

"Yes, teacher," I say. "I understand."

"Good girl."

Another smack—this one harder—hits my behind. I arch into the sensation. The sharp sting makes me gasp, but wetness floods my pussy when he spanks me again.

"Have I made myself clear on this issue? No talking back," Ethan says.

"I don't think so," I whisper, swaying my hips back and forth, wanting more the same way I want more of Warrick when his huge cock is hurting me in the best way. "I'm going to talk back to you again. I can't help myself."

The next stinging blow makes me cry out.

Callan twists my hair, and pain fills my scalp, too. There's something so satisfying about this pain, though, just like Warrick's roughness in bed.

"Tweak her nipples," Ethan demands.

With his back against the wall next to me, Callan's hands land on my breasts and squeeze. Then, he takes my nipples between his strong, calloused fingers and rolls each one into a tight bud.

The ache sends me soaring. I writhe into his touch, bringing my knees together to ease the ache between them.

"Stand how I told you," Ethan growls, whacking me again, even harder now. My bottom throbs with heat, as if my skin is burned. I whimper and spread my legs again.

Callan's warm hands caress my inner thighs. His fingers slide between my legs, pulling my panties aside and gliding up and down my folds. He sucks in a breath and growls low in his throat. His touch is such sweet relief, I want to cry. My pussy throbs with each stroke of his rough fingers.

Ethan growls, too, and another stinging blow lands on my skin. My body's on fire, caught between the intensity of the ruler and Callan's hands, teasing my breasts into a painful ache of need and then dipping into my panties again. I start to reach for Callan, but Ethan slaps me harder.

"Did I tell you to move?" he growls.

"No, sir."

"Hands against the wall until I say so." Ethan rises and places the measuring device on the chair.

I'm trembling with need as I stand in the perfect place, sandwiched between two of the strongest, most powerful mates. I can smell their arousal, the scent of sweat and musk of desire on them, and I want to scream with wanting them. Palms pressed into the plaster, my legs open wider as I writhe in place.

Ethan rubs my ass with sweet, tender caresses while ducks between me and the wall and sucks on my nipples.

I moan in pleasure.

Ethan uses his hand to slap my backside.

His palm stings my raw skin while he pushes his cock against my hip.

"I think you've earned your reward now, Miss Wolf," Ethan says. He withdraws and crosses the room to the bed.

Already, I miss him. I turn my head to see where he's going.

He plunks on the edge of the bed. "Come over here and sit on my cock, facing away from me. Then suck my brother's dick at the same time."

Saliva fills my mouth as I step toward him.

He turns me to face Callan, grabs my hips, and positions my wet folds over his rigid erection. Then, he guides me down his length.

We both groan as he fills my slick pussy to my depths.

Callan watches for only a moment, then grabs my hair and pulls me forward. He guides his cock into my mouth and begins to pump into me while Ethan thrusts into me from behind.

My ass feels inflamed from the whacks of the ruler and the slaps. But the stretch of Ethan's cock stirs me into an ecstatic frenzy. I seize Callan's cock with one hand and finger his balls with the other. Completely overwhelmed with sensation, I suck Callan and fuck Ethan.

We're all groaning and grunting with pleasure, the animal noises only fueling my heat and making me frantic for release as the room is filled with the scent of our arousal.

I can't hold back, and I start to come in a writhing cascade of ecstasy. I moan around Callan's cock, and he grips my head, and his hips pump wildly as he lets go into my mouth.

Ethan takes his cue and roars his release, hot streams flooding into my ecstatic core until we're one giant blur of bliss.

Afterward, Ethan pulls me onto the bed, and he, Callan, and I snuggle into a tangle of sheets and bedding.

I'm so happy, I could cry. But somehow, I still want more. I can't get enough of these men, of the life of contentment and joy we're making out here in the swamps together. Maybe it's possible to find happiness again after Mama, after all—and more than I ever had with her, more than I ever dreamed existed in the world. I fall asleep between the brothers, my spirit soaring with fulfillment.

Chapter Six

Axel

Standing in a circle of pack members in the clearing at Creebay Creek, I give them the news—Luna's been attacked again. Her life is in danger, and I need their help.

A few trees ripped from the earth and tossed on the ground lay scattered around us. The storm has passed, though, leaving us in a sultry heatwave. Sweat drenches my skin and pastes my clothing to my body. I wipe the dampness from my brow and continue. "The attack was brutal and unprovoked. She and Callan were out in the woods picking herbs, nothing to warrant such an attack. We've got to get to the bottom of this and find out why Luna is a target. And we've got to protect her. Are y'all willing to help?"

All around me heads nod in agreement.

"Absolutely," Adolpha says. "She and those triplets worked hard to repair my roof." Her gaze flits toward Warrick, who stands by my side.

A few of the others murmur their assent.

Return to the Pack

"You've got it, boss," Borris says, his arm around his wife, who holds their little girl. "I don't know what I would have done if you all hadn't come to my and my wife's rescue." He tugs her closer and kisses the top of the child's head.

For one brief, fleeting second, my chest clenches at their sweet family. I wonder if I'll ever give Luna pups, and a pang of restlessness stirs my insides. I'd like nothing more than to plant my seed inside my mate and start our own family. I haven't been able to get her out of my mind—nothing has worked. If anything, my intense bond with her has only grown stronger until I'm completely consumed. Seeing her wrecked and bleeding again brought out the most intense protective feelings I've ever had.

Warrick nudges me out of my fantasies as he addresses the group. "Whoever these wolves are, they're freaks. They're enormous and vicious, some sort of mutant wolves. Somehow they've been genetically altered to beast-like proportions. Maybe hopped up on goblin blood or…"

A few of the elders glance at each other, and I wonder if they're thinking about the same thing they told me—the unthinkable, unspeakable act of eating human flesh.

"But your brother managed to kill the one who attacked Luna, right?" Borris says.

Warrick's expression looks grim as he speaks. "He honestly doesn't know how he managed. He figured a burst of adrenaline gave him the strength he needed."

I cross my arms over my chest. "But what if that hadn't happened? Luna would be dead, and we'd be devastated. We've *got* to keep her safe. She's my mate." Rage rocks my soul at the thought of losing Luna to those crazed wolves. I already lost her once, and I won't do it again. "Right now, we've made her swear to not take a step out of the house unless accompanied by one of us, but that's obviously not a permanent solution."

"Where are you staying now that your house is destroyed and her house is still surrounded by water?" Adolpha asks.

"We're all out at our casa," Warrick states, matching my stance. "Our area didn't suffer the same damage as your street."

Adolpha scratches her head. "You're a ways out, and yet the beast-wolf found her. Do you think they were seeking her, or could it be a coincidence? Maybe they were just hunting in the woods and happened on her."

"It's the second time this has happened," I admit.

Like a lightning bolt, the sudden appearance of a vampire blurring into the center of the circle surprises everyone.

Borris's wife shrieks and clutches her little girl close.

Return to the Pack

Another vampire blurs into the clearing, and then another and another. Soon we're surrounded by the bloodsuckers.

And then all hell breaks loose as the vampires attack.

"Get to the truck," Borris shouts to his wife.

"Get the kids to safety!" Kato, my sentinel and also a parent, calls to his mate.

The rest of us shift into wolves and launch into the fight.

We're all tearing at one another's throats when another vampire—the bloodsucker known as Drake—blurs into the clearing and shouts, "Why are you destroying us? You broke your agreement."

There's a pause in the fray, and I shift into my human form.

"What are you talking about?" I demand. Giving away pack land to get Luna back from the vampires may not have been my most brilliant move, but I'm a man of my word. I always keep my agreements.

"You gave us land, and now you're killing us," Drake says coldly as he walks in a slow circle around me.

He's a big man, at least six foot six, but I'm not intimidated by him.

"Why would we do that?" I glance at the others of my pack, who now stare at us.

Blood stains their fur and faces.

The vampires we've been fighting gingerly feel their wounds. One of them runs his tongue along the inside of his mouth before spitting out a tooth. He gives a derisive snort and glares at me as if I'm the one who took out his tooth.

"Because you're all a bunch of animals," Drake says, coming to a stop before me and drawing himself up. "We can't trust you."

His bespoke suit clings to him like a second skin. The way he holds himself makes him look like royalty. For all I know, the asshole is the vampire prince.

"I may be a lot of things, but I'm not a liar," I growl. Blood drips down my cheek. I wipe it away with the back of my hand. "I gave you that property fair and square. Why would I turn around and kill you?"

"Tell them." Drake's hand sweeps toward Evan, one of the other vampires.

Evan, the asshole who took Luna before, bares his fangs. "We were attacked by wolves midday when we were all in repose. Then you same lying mutts attacked the humans we keep as food. Several of them are now *dead.*" He spits a mouthful of blood in the ground near my feet.

My brow furrows as I turn my attention toward my pack.

Several shake their heads, and another shrugs, indicating they don't know what the vampires are talking about either.

"We didn't do shit," I say, directing my attention back at Drake. "I have full knowledge of my pack."

"Liar," Evan snarls.

My body stiffens, and I'm about to launch at his throat when Drake reaches out his hand to touch Evan's shoulder.

"Let him speak," Drake says.

"When did this happen?" I demand.

"Over the last couple of days. We figured you're all desperate to get your land back since the storm took out many of your homes." Drake's eyes appear as cold as glaciers as he looks down his nose at me.

"And that speaks to the reason it couldn't have been us—our pack is all consumed with repairing and restoring the houses that the storm destroyed," I reply. "When would we have time to murder you or your food stock? Not to mention we have no quarrels with humans."

Drake's hands land on his hips. "Are you saying there's a rogue pack in the land?"

My skin prickles at the reminder of the wolf who attacked Luna. "I don't know," I say slowly. "I've been too busy dealing with the storm to stay abreast of other packs. Kato?" I nod at my sentinel, the spy of our team.

Kato's excellent at what he does, but he might have been too busy to have noticed other wolves in our territory. He pushes back his long, raven-haired mane from his face. "I've seen nothing. Since the storm has abated, I've patrolled the area when I could find the time, but I haven't seen any rogue wolves."

I lift my hand to my face and stroke my jaw. It's got to be those mutant wolves, and not only are they brutal, but they're sneaky, leaving no trace of their presence. "A mutant wolf attacked one of our own," I admit to Drake. "It was larger than any of our pack members, hopped up on some kind of drug, and brutal. It was the second attack on her life—she's the one who you caged." I lean toward Evan, rage in my eyes, remembering how I had to negotiate with the only thing I had left to get her back—by giving up pack land.

Drake's eyes narrow as he studies me. "Why should I believe you?"

"Why shouldn't you believe me? Have I done anything to make you not trust my pack or me? They weren't happy I gave you our land, yet they respected my wishes and left you alone. And yet, *you've* been the ones who have infringed on the boundaries of the land. Before the storm hit, the pack told me they've spied you in our land." I'm seething, but my demeanor is calm as I gaze into Drake's lifeless eyes. "Maybe it's *you* who haven't kept to your agreement."

Evan and the other vampires shift side to side, eyeing one another out of the corners of their cold, dead eyes.

Drake glares at them. "I'll speak to my clan. But that still leaves the issue before us. Who are these so-called mutant wolves?"

I make a quick toss of my head toward Kato, indicating he approach.

He steps toward me, his eyes inquiring. "What would you like me to do, Alpha?"

"Take time off the repair and restoration project. Get some of the others to help you scout around. We've got to find out who these wolves are and what their intention is. The bloodshed has to stop. We've got enough on our hands to deal with without having to worry about new enemies."

Kato nods.

I turn back to Drake. "We're going to get to the bottom of this. Those wolves concern us all. They're coming for Luna, my mate. And I won't let that happen."

Chapter Seven

Luna

Something is throbbing between my legs when I awaken—steamy heat, and a desire so strong I could move mountains to get it. It's not what I *want* to wake up to. I long for one of my lovers, some of my lovers, *all* of my lovers. And even then, I know it won't be enough.

What is going on with me?

Eyes still closed, I pat the tangled sheets on either side of me. There's no one here. When I drifted off to sleep, I was nestled between Callan and Ethan, and I was somewhat sated. But now I feel as if I haven't mated in years.

I'm sweating, so I kick the covers off and run my hand across my belly, ribs, and breasts. My skin feels like scorching silk. Touching myself makes me even hotter, so my hand finds its way between my legs, where I touch and caress the liquid heat between my folds.

The distant sound of the screen door thwacking, followed by bootsteps, has me on the alert. My hand stills in the wet slit between my legs.

Return to the Pack

Which one will come to fill my need? I open my eyes and prop myself up on my elbows.

The footsteps come closer.

I sit up and thrust out my chest as an invitation to whoever's about to enter.

Axel strides in the room, his head tipped back slightly as he sniffs the air. A delicious, feral expression crosses his chiseled face, making him look ten times more handsome than he already is. A slow smile forms on his face, and he licks his lips. "Well, isn't this a glorious day?" He whips his t-shirt over his head, revealing ridges of muscle.

It's then I realize he's bruised, scraped, and bloody.

"Axel! What happened?"

"It doesn't matter," he says. "It's nothing, just a scrape." His hands find his belt buckle, and he yanks his belt free.

"It looks like you need medical care," I say, rising onto my knees.

"What I need, my darling mate, is right in front of me." His jeans fall to the floor, and his buckle clinks against the hardwood. "It smells like you're in heat, and I'm ready to put a hundred pups in your sweet belly. This must be why you've been so eager to mate, to stay home and make a home. You're nesting."

I blink, stupefied. So, this is what it feels like to be in heat. Throbbing with desire so strong I could start a forest fire with it. I should have remembered from the time it happened before, but it's been so long, and I had no one to satisfy me then, so it was more torturous than pleasant.

Eyelids lowered, I crawl toward the end of the bed on my belly, my wolf eager to show her submission to our Alpha. "Am I?"

"As sure as I can smell, you're ready for breeding," Axel says, taking a long, deep sniff as he approaches me. His heavy, thick cock bobs with each step. He reaches for my head and massages my scalp with solid and sure fingers. I moan and lap at the head of his cock, practically whimpering with desire to have it inside me.

As he caresses me, I rub my cheek against his muscular thigh, letting my lips skim along his shaft. "I'm listening."

"The question is…."

"Yes, Alpha?"

"Are you ready to produce an heir?" His hands move down to my back, where he kneads and massages.

Sweet swamp dogs, if I could purr, I'd be purring strong. "Yes," I say, shivering with pleasure.

"Then I'm going to breed you," Axel says as his hands move around to cup my breasts. He tweaks my nipples, and slick trickles down my thighs. "You're preparing to have a baby, and I'd be honored to father our children."

I don't know why but this statement has me all gushy inside. I slide my cheek across his thigh and nuzzle his balls with my nose, inhaling the musky heat radiating from him.

"Fuck, Luna," Axel breathes. "If I didn't want to shoot my seed inside of you, I'd come all over your face right now."

"I don't mind, as long as you come inside me afterward." I grab his thick erection between my hands and fit my mouth over the swollen head. Sucking, I hum and moan with desire.

"Fuck yeah," Axel growls as his hands find my scalp again, rubbing and caressing. "I'm going to fill you with so much come you can't hold it all."

I work his cock with my mouth and my tongue, so hungry I could scream. My hands grow slippery from my saliva and his pre-cum, and they glide up and down his stiff length.

Axel cups the back of my head and stops my slide and glide. "Get on your back, my love. I want to worship my True Mate like the goddess she is."

"I want that, too," I say, releasing my grip. I pivot on my hands and knees and arch my rump toward him.

"Oh, yes," he says, sliding his finger along my wet silk. "Just like that. You're so beautiful, Luna. Your body is my heaven."

He spreads me open and drops to his knees beside the bed, his mouth latching onto my pussy. He sucks the nectar from me, moaning and lapping up every drop. When he plunges his tongue inside me, I cry out, my body electrified as my walls clench in spasms and an orgasm wracks my body. Sweat breaks out over my skin, and I cry out his name, bucking and pushing my bottom against his face.

He groans and gives one last suck before standing. He spreads me open and thrusts deep inside my dripping pussy. "My turn," he growls, gripping my hips and slamming into me again.

It feels so good I can't even think, and helpless moans and whimpers escape as he pounds his thick, bare cock into my thirsty core.

"Touch yourself," he says, seizing my hips. "I want you to come hard on my cock when I knot up inside you." He doesn't move, but I can feel him quivering inside of me.

Grabbing a pillow from the head of the bed, I position it beneath me and press my right cheek into it. It smells like me, Callan, and Ethan. *Pure bliss.* I draw in our scent, rest my shoulder on the soft mattress and reach for my clit. Fingering myself, I start to moan as pleasure shoots through me.

Axel grinds his hips, slowly thrusting in and out while his fingers dig into my skin. His cock pulses with each thrust. "Is my little mate making herself feel good?" he murmurs.

"Yes," I breathe. The feelings pouring through me are exquisite, and I find I want to ride them, ride the wave of sensation without falling over the edge. My mind expands into a slow-motion drift. I can't believe it's possible to feel this good. My wolf is howling with bliss, with joy, with the strength of our connection. Even with the True Mate bond severed, she never stopped believing we were meant to be. Now we both believe it, and so does he.

I know Axel feels it, too. We're caught in the sensations of his bare cock owning every inch of my throbbing heat, riding a river of ecstasy so wild and free it could unravel us.

I'm aware of sounds, of Axel's soft grunts each time he thrusts into me, the songbirds outside the window, distant laughter like my other men are nearby, the comforting knowledge that we're all home, where we belong. And then there's the slick slide of Axel's cock as it claims me over and over again.

As I circle my clit with my fingertips, the sensation builds. I can feel Axel's cock expanding inside me with each thrust as his knot forms, stretching me until I can hardly take it. I want to milk this moment of glorious presence with Axel. We've become one driving need, and I can't tell where the boundaries of him and I are. There are none. We are one.

"I'm stuck," Axel growls. "I've fully knotted inside you. You're going to have to come to release me."

The feeling of pleasure continues to build as I feel myself stretched to the brink around the thick, fist-like knot at the base of his cock. When he tries to pull back even a bit, I shriek with pleasure and a little pain. I'm so full I think I'll tear open, and it's so sweet I can't help the tears that stream from my eyes as pure erotic energy streams through my system.

"Fucking come," Axel growls. "Come for your Alpha, my little mate."

Axel's thrusts have ceased, but I can feel his thick cock throbbing inside me.

My fingers circle around and around my swollen bud, faster and faster, until I explode. An animalistic cry pours from my throat as I let go around Axel's cock, my walls gripping him in their greedy hunger. He roars and bucks, calling my name as his seed bursts from him, planting deep inside me where they belong.

Another wave hits me, and hot fire shoots up my spine. I lose all sense of time and place. We're a cosmic explosion, exploding stars, one big mystery moment of fulfillment. Dimly, I'm aware of collapsing onto the mattress, with Axel falling with me, still inside, his knot holding us together.

Return to the Pack

We roll to the side and spoon, with his arm draped around my chest, making small strokes against my skin.

We lay here for quite some time, savoring the moment of mutual orgasm. I feel his knot begin to shrink again until at last he draws back and slips out of me.

"I think I put a whole litter of pups in you," he murmurs at last, sliding a protective hand around my belly.

"What are you talking about?" I say, rolling over to face him.

His eyes look soft and inviting as he gazes at me. "You're so beautiful, Luna."

"Are you saying you're ready for more?" I say in a low, sleepy voice. "Because I sure am."

Axel rubs his scruffy chin against my shoulder. "I can certainly oblige you," he says, and sure enough, I feel the stirrings of his arousal. "But the others might be jealous."

"Why would they be jealous?" I throw my leg over his hip and push my pussy against him.

"Because I just planted my flag first," he says, laughing. "It's a guy thing. We always like to be the first to claim the mountain."

"Oh, so now I'm a mountain?" I say, tweaking one of his nipples with my fingers.

"You're going to be soon enough. Your belly will grow with my baby inside."

"Will it?" I say, looking down at my flat abdomen.

"Yes," he says, and an adorable expression lights up his face.

Outside the window, the brothers' voices grow louder, like they're approaching the house. The tromp of their footsteps along the sand and gravel gets me all hot and bothered again.

"And will your seed be the victor?" I say, stroking his biceps.

"It's hard to say. I'll breed you until it happens, though.," Axel says, rolling me onto his back.

The backdoor squeaks open and bangs shut, and footsteps fill the house.

"They're going to smell your heat, too." He grabs his stiffening cock and slides it up and down my crack. "They'll want to breed you as well."

"They will?" I spread my legs wide.

"We all will," he says, his eyelids fluttering closed as he continues to stroke. "They'll breed you the same way I did. There's no mistaking the scent of a woman in heat, and we'll all make sure you have pups. Between the four of us, you'll be fat with babies, alright."

"Did I hear the word 'heat?'" Callan calls from just outside the room.

I'm going to have so much fun making babies with them all!

Chapter Eight

Ethan

"Time to make some babies," I yell, pushing past Callan and heading for the bedroom. The scent of Luna's arousal fills the whole damn house.

Callan and Warrick are right behind me, stripping off their clothes the same way I am. We burst into the bedroom to see Axel grinding into Luna.

When he hears us, he rolls off her and grins at us, his cock standing proud and slick with Luna's juices. "I got here first," he says smugly. "My seed has already been planted."

Luna's legs are spread, revealing her dripping pussy to the rest of us. It looks swollen and needy, practically begging us to fuck her, and the smell makes my head spin, my wolf roaring to leap out and fuck the tarnation out of her.

"It only paved the way for my seed," I say, leaping onto the bed next to Luna.

Luna lets out a squeal and a giggle.

"Which will pave the way for mine," Callan says, jumping on top of me.

"Y'all all know whose seed is the biggest, the baddest, and the strongest," Warrick gruffs, shoving between us all.

"Which one of us is the Alpha here?" Axel says, but he's grinning as he scoots over, tucking an arm behind his head and watching us kissing and licking and touching our little mate. She may not be our True Mate, but she's our treasured mate, the one we chose and our wolves chose, and we worship her body with ours.

I can't wait to breed her, to watch her swell with a litter of pups, to hold our child in my arms. The fierceness of this thought surprises me. I can't say I've longed to be a father before. If anything, I wanted nothing to do with fatherhood since we were raised by a bastard. I know all my brothers feel the same way—about our father, and maybe, about being a father to Luna's progeny. But with her, everything is different.

The moment this sweet, innocent little whisp of a girl walked into our woods, our lives changed, and there's no changing back. We wouldn't go back if we could.

"I'm next," I say, staking my claim and moving between Luna's thighs. My dick's rigid and ready to stake our claim—me and my wolf both.

"Want to bet?" Callan says, jostling my shoulder.

"Boys, boys, you can all get a turn," Luna says. She spreads her legs wide and pushes her hips up, an invitation that shuts us all up as we stare at the juicy offering.

"And that's my cue," Axel says, rolling off the bed. "I'll stand guard to ensure that no mutant wolves are sniffing around."

"Maybe they could smell her heat was coming," I offer. "Maybe that's why he attacked her."

"That's the last thing we need—a mutated wolf catching the scent of Luna in her hours of need and coming for her again," Axel mutters, pulling on his jeans. "I'll watch. You fuck."

"Damn straight," Callan says. "If our mate has a need to be quenched, that's our job." He turns Luna's face toward his and plants a hungry kiss on her lips.

Axel departs, and we all engage in a free-for-all fuck fest. A wolf in heat is the definition of insatiable, and I know she'll keep needing us to breed her until her heat subsides in a few days. Until then, we'll all fuck her until we're raw and she's so sore she can't walk straight.

I'm up for the challenge.

True to her word, Luna gives us each a turn to shoot our loads in her sweet pussy. Warrick goes first, but Luna doesn't neglect us. She jerks us off while Warrick drills her into the bed. I fuck her next, riding her with a fury until she comes hard again. I keep dipping down to taste her succulent lips, overwhelmed with the love I feel for this wolf who is barely more than a pup herself, but who can take the most brutal poundings from all three of us.

At last, Callan's patience wears out, and he's overcome. I've barely finished squeezing the last drops of cum into her scalding pussy when he yanks me off her, flips her over, and drives into her hard and fast from behind. She moans and writhes and gasps, and Warrick shoves his cock into her mouth, already hard again from watching us fuck her.

I'm already getting hard watching my brothers take our mate from both ends. When Callan's done, Warrick and I pounce and share her between us this time. We keep fucking until Luna taps out, and then we fall into a sweaty, exhausted pile. I don't know how much time has gone down, and I don't really care.

We lie about in the aftermath for a while, dozing peacefully until Warrick rolls from the bed and pads from the room. I'm sure he's going for a smoke.

Callan's on his back with his arm thrown over his face, and Luna's settled on her belly between Callan and me with her eyes closed.

"Are you asleep?" I ask, stroking her side.

"Not yet," she says in a sleepy voice. "But I'm so tired."

"We definitely tired you out," I say, crawling up to prop my head on a pillow. "You'll be up and ready for more in the morning, though. A wolf in heat… The devil himself couldn't be more greedy."

"I'm greedy?" she asks, her lids fluttering open.

"In the best way," I say. "I fucking love it. And don't worry, we'll sate you all day and night until you're so stuffed full of cum you can't help but get pregnant."

Callan snorts out a laugh.

I coil a lock of Luna's hair around my fingers. "Have you thought about where we're going to live?"

"We're living here," Luna says, lifting her gaze to mine. "Can't we stay here?"

"Sure," I say. "We don't have a problem with you and Axel here, but if it was tight when you lived here, it's even tighter now with the two of you."

"What are you saying?" Luna says, a frown marring her features. She crawls up next to me and snuggles into my side.

Callan rolls over and hooks his leg over hers. "We were talking about it earlier when we were outside. We need bigger digs."

"Bigger digs?" Luna asks.

"Digs is another way to say house," I explain as I tuck my arm under her head and pull her close, kissing the top of her mussed hair.

"Can we build on this land?" Luna asks.

"We have the land to do that, sure," I say. "But Axel won't want to live this far from the pack. Now that we're in, Warrick won't either. And you'll be more protected if we're living near the pack. That way they can watch out for you, and you don't have to have an escort when you leave the house. They'll know the moment an outsider steps onto pack land, and they'll come to your defense."

As much as I like living out here, Luna's safety is the most important thing. And once she has pups, keeping them safe will be at the top of the list, too.

Luna places her palm on my belly. I can practically see the wheels turning in her head.

Warrick strides into the room with a cigarette balanced between his fingers. He perches by the open window and blows a stream out through the crack. "What are y'all talking about?" he asks, a frown creasing his brow. "You look serious."

"We were talking about what to do when Luna's with child," I tell him.

Warrick chuckles. "The swimmers of four potent males are all duking it out right now, vying for dominance. One of us will fill her womb this heat." He takes another drag from his smoke. "I'm sure it will be mine."

"Asshole," I say. "It could be any of us."

"Hey, Alpha," Warrick calls out, pushing the window wide.

"Yeah?" calls Axel's voice from the edge of the woods.

"Get on over here," Warrick calls through a lungful of smoke. "There's a serious talk going on that you need to be a part of."

A minute later, Axel props his forearms on the windowsill. "What's up?"

"We need a bigger house for all the pups Luna's going to pop out," I say. "No way can we all live here." I extend my hand to Warrick, indicating I want a drag of his cigarette. I quit years ago, but every once in a while, I still get the urge.

He hands it over, and I bring it to my lips and inhale, taking a long, deep draw before handing it back. A stream of blueish smoke leaves my lungs, and the nicotine buzz fills my bloodstream.

"So, what are you thinking?" Axel says.

"There's no fucking way I can live without these assholes," I say, nodding at each of my brothers. "We're a family, you know?"

"And us?" Axel asks, raising a brow.

I shrug. "Yeah, you're right. Maybe you're family now, too."

The only people I've ever called family are Warrick and Callan. Now, I'm claiming Luna and Axel as part of my tribe.

Axel nods. "Even though we all joked about who gets the rights to claim fatherhood to Luna's child, it doesn't matter which one of us gives her pups. We'll all be the fathers."

"Fuck yeah, we will," Warrick growls. "All I care about is that our baby-girl's needs get satisfied, and she gets what she wants."

"Same here," Callan says, opening his eyes.

"I wouldn't have it any other way," Axel says. "As long as we're all in agreement as to who got there first." He winks, and a cocky grin splits his face.

"Fuck off," Warrick says, but he's grinning, too. He grinds his cigarette out on the windowsill and flicks it outside.

"We haven't heard from you, Luna. What are your thoughts?" Axel asks, gazing at her with the same soft gaze we probably all have right now.

Luna stretches her toes and gives a big yawn, her body still flushed with the afterglow of all the orgasms we gave her. "I want to be a family more than anything."

"Me too," I say, squeezing her to my side.

She looks at each one of us in turn. "I don't ever want us to fight again about anything. We've all had our upsets with our first families. Do you think we can agree to be the loving families none of us ever had?"

I don't know about the others, but the way she regards us with all that innocence she carries makes me all choked up. It's like someone stuck a candle inside my ribcage. "I'm down with that," I say gruffly.

Her eyes start to mist over. "Thank you," she whispers.

"Same here," Callan says, and she trains her gaze on him.

"I'm in," says Warrick, tipping his chin at us.

"Then we're all in agreement," Axel says. He pushes away from the window. "Let's make it official. As soon as you're out of heat, let's perform a commitment ceremony in front of the pack. We'll get it all out in the open and get their blessing. Hopefully."

"We will," Luna assures us, her voice sleepy even as she rolls over and arches her back, pushing her ass against me to show me she's ready for another round.

Damn if I'm not the happiest guy in the world as I oblige her.

Chapter Nine

Luna

What a week it's been! I don't think I've moved from the bedroom once, except to pee and shower. Callan even brought me my meals in bed, with each of my men taking turns feeding me and waiting on me hand and foot, since they insist my only job for the week is to get a baby in my belly. When I'm not eating or cuddling with my four mates, I'm engaged in various forms of what Ethan calls 'sexual satisfaction.'

The mating urge has me in its grips for a solid week, and I can't say I don't enjoy being fucked every which way by my four strong, wild wolves until I beg for mercy, and then doted on in turn. They keep feeding me and encouraging me to work up my stamina so they can all go again, sometimes taking turns and sometimes all pouncing and pleasuring me at once until I feel so good I think I'll die. I feel like some sort of demon who can never get enough, who wants nothing more than to suck the lifeforce out of her men through their cocks and into her womb.

Return to the Pack

But not one of them complained. They were all too happy to feed my hungry womb with their seed over and over again, even propping my hips up on pillows afterwards to keep it from running out.

By the time it's over, a new bond hums between us. I can sometimes even sense the invisible threads that bind us all together—we're well and truly a family.

Today, I'm stepping away from the house with all my men by my side. Now that my heat's abated, Axel made arrangements for a pack ceremony to swear us all in as official Jacksonville pack members. Additionally, Warrick will be sworn in as Axel's Second in Command.

As I sit in Axel's truck, snuggled between him and Callan, a sense of contentment I've never experienced before settles over my being. The sun is shining, the storm has passed, and we've survived. More than that, my heat brought us all together, and now we're well and truly bound as a family. I'm proud of my role in it, proud that I'm the one who ended the feud between the outlaw triplets and the pack, and proud that my heat got the triplets and Axel so comfortable with each other, as it's hard to be standoffish when you're all naked and bumping up against each other.

Warrick and Ethan are behind us on their motorcycles, ready to ride. They exchange a nod at one another, and then each man pulls on either side of the truck.

Axel turns to look at Warrick through the open window.

"Is that the fastest you can drive, old man?' Warrick yells, his long hair whipping behind him.

It's going to take me days to comb out the tangles in his hair, but neither of us will care, although Warrick will surely pretend to be grumpy about it.

"Who you calling an old man?" Axel calls back, gunning the truck.

"We're calling you old," Ethan hollers from the other side of the truck, through Callan's open window. He recently cut his hair short, nearly to the scalp, so no tangles for him. "You drive like my grandpa when he was stoned."

He lets out a laugh as he slows the bike to a crawl, falling behind. Then, in a burst, he leans on the throttle, and he's by our side again. The roar of their engines sends a thrill through my spine, and the smell of the exhaust makes me feel free, like I do when I'm on the bike with one of them.

Ethan looks through the cab at Warrick, and they each exchange another nod.

Then, in unison, they roar in front of us, leaving us in the dust.

"So that's what we're playing at, is it?" Axel grumbles. Then he floors the gas pedal.

Return to the Pack

I let out a squeal, but in truth, I love being wild and free with my men. The swamp blurs as we speed along the dusty road, with Warrick's and Ethan's taillights ahead.

"Flash your tits at them," Axel says, giving me a mischievous grin.

Callan chuckles and pulls me up onto his lap. When we get close, I lean my head and torso out the window, lifting my t-shirt to reveal my pale breasts with their nipples still red and raw from all the sucking they got over the past week. I swear Warrick and Ethan are going to get in a wreck when they start to swerve, staring hard at me in their rearview mirrors.

I'm laughing so hard I nearly fall out the window. Callan's hands firmly clutch my hips, keeping me inside as his body quakes with laughter.

Warrick falls back next to Axel's windows once more. "You've got an unfair advantage in your truck, Alpha."

"Secret weapon," Axel says with a smirk. He rests his hand on my bare thigh as I settle between them again, and Warrick and Ethan fall back behind the truck again.

When we arrive at the clearing, the other pack members are already there and are prepping the fire pit for a barbecue. But my gaze lands with a jolt on the one person I'd hoped to never see again in this lifetime—Elder Amexaryl.

Looking as frail as ever, like she might blow away if the wind catches her, Elder Amexaryl stands among the other older members of the pack. She's the old crone who severed the True Mate connection between Axel and me. In so doing, she left my heart a shredded, bloody mess and the True Mate mark which had appeared during our bonding ceremony nothing but a faded scar. It's still that way, and it will never glow with the moonlight magic that shows the world that I belong to Axel and he belongs to me.

"What's she doing here?" I hiss at Axel, my wolf whining down in her belly at the sight of the offending elder.

Axel winces and casts a guilty look in my direction. "She's our ceremonial elder. Only she can perform the ritual of a pack bond."

"She's the one who severed our connection, Axel. She *broke* me. And now you want her to welcome us into the pack? Oh, no. Take me home." I wish I weren't sitting between two strong men, or I'd have bolted for the woods already. My wolf is crying to race away in fear at the reminder of how dangerous the elder is to us.

Warrick, who's parked his bike next to Ethan's, strides toward the truck. "Is there a problem?" he demands, eyeing my face with concern through the driver's window.

"I'll say." I lift my hand and stab the air in the elder's direction. "*She's* the one who broke our True Mate bond. And supposedly she's the one who's going to forge the pack bond between us all."

Warrick studies Axel. "Is this true?"

"I'm afraid so," Axel says, appearing glum. "She's a revered elder in the pack. Magic runs through her veins. She's conducted all ceremonies in the pack since before I was a pup."

"And you didn't think to inform Luna?" Warrick rests his hands on the sill of the window and glowers at Axel.

"No," he growls back. "This is how the pack works. Sometimes, we do things we don't like for the sake of others. An Alpha most of all."

"Let me handle this, baby girl," Warrick says to me. "Wait here." He casts one more glare at Axel before striding toward the elder while I try to shrink inside the truck seat.

"Not your best move, Alpha," Callan says.

"Shut the fuck up," Axel snaps, but his expression looks wretched. He turns to me and pierces me with his aquamarine eyes. "I'm sorry, Luna. Honestly, it escaped my mind, what with everything that's gone on of late. And she's a part of the pack. It's not her fault that I had her perform that ceremony."

"I don't like her," I say in a quavering voice. All the pain of this past year floods my body, erasing this last joyous week of bonding. It's as if a fire of hurt burns through me—a fire that I thought I'd extinguished. It burns up my heart and my wolf soul at once.

Several paces off, Warrick and the elder are having what looks like a heated exchange. Some of the other pack members have stopped their preparations and are staring at them. Finally, Warrick leads Elder Amexaryl in our direction.

"I don't want to talk to her. Don't make me talk to her," I say, seizing Callan's arm.

"Just hear what she has to say," Callan soothes.

My heart's beating so fast as the elder reaches the truck, I think it's going to shoot from my throat and my wolf shoot from my skin. Still clinging to Callan's arm, I clutch Axel's hand, too, needing even more reassurance.

Elder Amexaryl peers in the window as her wispy gray hair billows about her head, caught by the breeze. Her pale, almost white-colored eyes feel as if they're probing my soul. "Child," she says in her quavering voice. "Would you be so kind as to step out of the truck? It seems we have a few things to discuss."

"No!" I blurt and bear down on Callan's arm and Axel's hand.

Elder Amexaryl steps back as if I've agreed and waits for Axel to open the door.

He extricates his hand from my grip and slides from the front seat, holding his hand out to me. *He's* a good pack member, respecting the rules and order of the pack system.

I'm not. I press into Callan.

"Go on, Luna. We're here to protect you. No one lays a hand on my mate or I'll rip her head from her body myself," he assures me in a low growl.

The ghosts of past pain nearly split me in two. I shake my head. "I don't want to."

"Luna. Do as requested," Axel commands, still holding his hand out to me. But he doesn't use his wolf dominance to force me, and I hold onto the relief in that. He could make me obey, especially because the pack is here to witness my rebellious behavior, but he lets me know he trusts me so he doesn't have to. My wolf trusts him, and she urges me to obey our Alpha like a good wolf. "If you don't like what she says, we'll make other arrangements."

"Are you just saying that to get me out of the truck?" I ask.

"No. I give you my word," Axel says, his gaze as open and unguarded as the sky above him.

With trepidation, I reach for his hand and let him tug me out of the vehicle. I grip his hand and haul him with me to step before the elder. As I study her, my wolf notices she doesn't look so tough. We're young and healthy. We could take her.

The corners of her lips curve in her wrinkled face as if she can read my thoughts. "Child, my role in this pack is to do as I must... Nothing more, nothing less. It's a role passed down through generations. My mother, and my mother's mother, and her mother before all shared the same gift."

"You almost *destroyed* me!" I cry, unable to hold back the howl of pain my wolf feeds my heart at the reminder of the anguish we experienced at her hand.

"I didn't do that. Your Alpha did," she says, her gaze moving from me to Axel and back.

Axel's hand gives mine a reassuring squeeze. He said the same—that it's his fault, not hers. But I love him now. I forgave him. The pain remains, though, at least a part of it, like the scar on my arm that reminds me of what he did.

"I'm here to rejoin you in a new configuration," the elder says. "It won't be like before, as you'll never be True Mates again. But you can still be a part of the pack, and one day, you and Axel can be mated if you wish."

"You can't take the others away from me!" I feel just like a child wailing at Mama because she spanked me.

"Nor would I ever—unless you declared your intention to be mated to one of them." Her gaze appears timeless like all her fore-mothers speak through her.

By now, the other pack members have gathered around us. Kato, Adolpha, Borris, his wife and child, and others solemnly witness our exchange. The elder leads us to the center of the clearing, and the rest of the pack forms a circle around us, their faces solemn as they wait for our induction. The breeze picks up into a gust that blows leaves, sand, and other debris into the air.

"Do any of you desire to be less than a fully bonded member of the Jacksonville pack?" she asks, turning her head to gaze at Axel and the triplets.

The brothers all shake their heads and come to stand beside me.

In a loud, clear voice, Axel says, "I was a fool before. I have paid my penance, and I'll continue to pay it through lifetimes to be mated to Luna. She is my soul. It is my honor to welcome her and these men into our pack, to share what we have equally as we do with all members."

"This bond shall serve you well, Luna, dear," Elder Amexaryl assures me. "Once it is done, you and the rest of the pack shall be as one. You'll share a telepathic bond. Each of you shall know when the other is in danger. Each of you shall know when the prey has been spotted or when the other is needed. You will not need words to communicate." She pauses, and the air around us stills as if waiting for my answer.

The words lodge in my throat, however. I can still feel the sting of the past slicing through my heart. I don't ever want to experience their rejection again.

"I understand you are being hunted," Elder Amexaryl says, reaching for my hands.

I let her enfold them in her warm, papery touch. Instantly, a deep sense of calm flows through me. "Yes," I say. "I am."

"The beasts that hunt you are evil. They're no longer wolves but aberration to the species."

The word "evil" is like a punch to the gut, and I try to yank my hands away from Elder Amexaryl.

Her fingers harden into claws, not letting me go. As she does this, I'm filled to overflowing with a kind of strength I've never before experienced. I feel as powerful as all of my lovers combined, and I know this strength comes from the pack... Joining together gives us all the power of many.

Elder Amexaryl holds me in her steady gaze, letting the preview of what I'll have fade. "If you choose to accept, this bond will be protect you in case of further attacks, more necessary now than ever. It's your choice if you want to be a member of the pack, though, Luna. All you have to do is say yes."

The wind picks up again, and it seems to swirl around us, embracing us in a sphere of magical possibilities.

Say yes.

Return to the Pack

The words seem to flow into my brain from Axel, and my wolf calms, eagerness building inside her where fear and loneliness and distrust have resided all my life.

We accept you. We're ready.

These words flow from Axel, but somehow I know they're flowing from the pack, the only way they can reach me—through my bond with Axel.

"Then, yes, yes, *yes,*" I say, and my heart swells as my wolf dances with happiness. I sweep my gaze at each pack member. "Please accept me into your pack. Accept us all."

"I accept," Kato says, raising his fist high.

"As do I!" Aldopha states, lifting her fist into the air.

One by one, each pack member states their assent.

I'm buzzing with energy, buoyed by this sense of community I've never had before.

"It is done, child," Elder Amexaryl says, touching my forehead with her fingertip. She bows her head slightly and withdraws.

All around me, there are whoops and cheers. Hands clap me on the back, arms embrace me, and I feel folded into the pack, welcomed with open arms.

Then Elder Amexaryl repeats the performance for Callan, Ethan, and then Warrick. At the end, she goes on to swear him in as Second in Command. Then there are more hugs and cheers. When the congratulations cease, and people start to drift toward the fire pit to get the meat on the grill, Axel pulls me aside.

"What is it?" I say, gazing at him. My heart swells with love for the wolf-man standing before me. He is well and indeed my mate, even if our marks no longer glow. The bond of the pack only confirms it.

"I'm so proud of you, Luna." He looks at me with a fire in his eyes I've never seen. He takes my hands in his, and our gazes tangle.

"Are you?" I say, my heart pitter-pattering in my chest.

"Extremely. And…" He licks his lips and swallows. "I'm so in love with you, I can barely breathe at times. I don't care if we have a True Mate bond. You're my mate, as I am yours. It's always been this way. I believe my wolf spirit has returned to Earth, again and again, countless times, to find you and be with you."

Tears of joy fill my eyes. "I feel it, too, Axel. Maybe we were scared of the bond when we did it before. Maybe you had to sever the bond to prove that it's real and true and right."

His eyes are shining as he listens to me. "Maybe," he says in a choked voice. "I'll never stop regretting that I hurt you, though. I'll never stop making it up to you. Not in this lifetime or the next."

I can't believe how happy I am to be bonded with the pack, with the triplets, with Axel. And yet, in the back of my mind, there's a tiny whispering voice of warning that tells me our family's bond will be tested. I can only hope we all make it through the test intact, because I have a feeling we'll be adding one more to our family soon.

Chapter Ten

Callan

"Fuck this shit," I say, staring at the dump of a house before us. "This place is a rat-infested dump. Wait, a rat-infested dump would be better than this shit-hole."

The two-story derelict house, built on stilts to survive a flood, is so severely in need of repair inside and out that it should be condemned. It's surrounded by palm trees that managed to survive the hurricane—they're the nicest looking parts of this property. Across the street, lumber and debris float in Goblin Creek. It'll take months for the waterways to clear the remnants of houses the wind scooped into its greedy paws. Golden Glade Street, where most of the pack lives, is even worse, or we'd just rebuild where Axel's house was. Luna's is too small, and ours is in no way built to accommodate a child.

The mealy-mouthed property owner of the house on Holiday Lane shifts side to side on his spindly legs. He's not a pack member, just one of the many humans who take advantage of the Jacksonville pack however they can. In this case, it's by charging an exorbitant amount of money for a house that should have been blown away by the storm of a couple of weeks ago.

He starts to say something about how low he can go, but I stopped listening to him when we stepped from the truck. I throw my arm around Luna and guide her back to my bike.

Her face is a study in disappointment. I hate to see that look on her face, and I'll do anything to change it into one of happiness. "The next place will be better—you'll see."

I hand her the helmet we insist she wear when riding on the back of our motorcycles. While we could give a rat's ass about motorcycle riding laws, she's precious cargo.

"This is the fifteenth house we've looked at," she whines, frowning as she dons the helmet. "They're all either too expensive or falling apart like this place. We'll never find the right place that accommodates all of us. Let's just go home. I'm tired and hot."

I hesitate for a moment. There's got to be something I can do to turn that frown into a smile. The day is like a wet blanket we can't throw off, though, so she's right about that part. The heat's making us all grumpy lately, but I have a feeling Luna's hormones have something to do with it. Which means we need to get a baby-friendly house, stat.

An idea surfaces, and I snap my fingers.

"What?" she asks, swatting away a handful of mosquitos.

"I'll tell you back at the house." I swing my leg over the bike and grab the handlebars.

"Will I like it?" she asks, clambering on the back. She wraps her hands around my midsection.

I wrap my forearm over her arm, hugging her to me. "I think you will," I say before powering up the engine. I guide the bike onto the street, and we're away.

Back at the house, I hold Luna's hand as we stroll toward the porch. I love having a mate—strike that—I love having Luna as my mate. Sharing her with my brothers and Axel might seem funny to an outsider, but it's natural for us. I've been sharing women with my brothers all my life, so it makes sense when we find one worth keeping, we all get to enjoy her. Adding Axel wasn't even odd for us, since we're used to sharing. Maybe to him it was, but to me, it's like we're all made to be together.

Entering through the screen door, we find the others sitting around the kitchen table. Empty plates sit before them, and they're all talking about some shit or another.

"Any luck?" Axel says to me, popping the last bit of a taco into his mouth.

"Not a bit of luck, but an idea hit me." I release Luna's hand, and she wanders toward Warrick, who pats his lap in invitation.

"Did it hurt?" Ethan asks, smirking. He lifts the bottle of beer before him to his lips and empties it.

I flash him my middle finger, pull a chair out, turn it around, and straddle it.

"What's your idea?" Axel says, leaning back in his seat. He casts an assessing gaze at Luna as if to make sure she's still here, still intact.

"You're the pack leader, right?" I say, resting my arms on the chair back.

Axel frowns at me and nods, waiting to see where I'm going with this.

"So, shouldn't you be given some extra privileges, like your choice of land to rebuild on? We're finding nothing but rundown houses or expensive bullshit homes. We can't live in a dump with a baby, and we don't need to break our backs to afford something with a pool only a rich prick can live in."

I know I sound like my dad right now, but it's the truth.

"A pool might be nice," Luna says, who's snuggling into Warrick's arms. "I like swimming."

Axel's head cocks to the side like he's contemplating what I just said. "You're thinking to build?"

"Yeah," I say. "That way, we could give Luna the perfect house that meets everyone's needs. Room for all the pups we want to raise, on a piece of land where they can run and hunt, not on Golden Glade, where it's in town. A wolf should be able to roam."

Axel tips his chair back and stares up at the ceiling. His eyes have clouded over, so I know I've hit on something worth considering.

"There's a perfect clearing in the old hunting grounds that was deeded to me when I became Alpha. I never needed it since I already owned the house in town, and I wanted to live among the pack," he says.

"Let's go out and take a look at it today," I say, sitting tall, excitement winding through me. "We can start making plans to build right away if we're all in favor."

Axel huffs out a sigh. "There's a problem."

"What is it? Septic? Electric? Putting in a well? We can find someone to do all that." My stomach growls, and I realize Luna, and I haven't eaten all day. "You hungry, Luna? I'll fix us supper."

"You finish with your talk. I'll make us some tacos. Is there any leftover meat?"

"The wolf whose lap you're sitting in ate the last chunk." Ethan hops to his feet. "I'll make you two some spaghetti."

We've all taken to jumping up in service when Luna needs anything. She's our mate, carrying one of our heirs, after all. That's the only job she needs to be doing right now.

"Thanks, Ethan," she says, flashing him a heart-melting smile.

We've all turned into pussy-whipped versions of our badass selves since Luna arrived, but none of us are complaining. When the pussy's that good, it's worth it.

As Ethan heads to the cupboard for noodles, Axel says, "It's not as simple as that."

"What's the complicated part?" I scratch the back of my head. "We make plans, we build it. How hard is that? Does our Alpha not know how to get his hands dirty?"

Axel doesn't rise to the bait. Instead he blows out a long breath of air and crumples his paper napkin into a ball. "It's part of the property I gifted to the vamps."

"Shit," Warrick says.

"Oh, Axel," Luna says, her lavender doe-eyes going wide. "You did that to get me back. It's my fault."

"It's not," he growls.

"Fuck," I say. "Can we get it back?"

Axel's face pulls into a scowl. "Since the vampires attacked us the other day, what's your best guess to the answer to that question?"

"Yeah, that's a negative," Warrick says. "We barely calmed them down. They think we're killing off the humans they use for feeding stations. No peace negotiations happening there anytime soon." He lowers his head to nibble Luna's neck.

She arches her back and makes a humming noise that arouses my cock. I remember what it felt like when she hummed around my dick this morning.

Dragging my attention back to the conversation, I say, "So what are our options? Is there another piece of property we can use?"

Axel rises from the table and begins stacking dishes. With his arms laden, he heads for the sink. "There are, but none like that. That would have been perfect, our own little paradise on pack land, but away from prying eyes."

"Away from the nosy pack gossips hearing us make Luna scream every night," Ethan says with a grin, running his hand over his beard.

"Well, we need to find something," I say, casting him a dark look. "Can you imagine all of us crowded into this house with a baby to boot?"

"And what if she has twins or triplets?" Warrick asks, lighting up a cigarette.

"Then double or triple shit," I say.

We're going to have to find a solution. We want nothing more than Luna's happiness. None of us want to be stepping on one another's toes living here or trekking through diapers filled with baby shit. We're already overcrowded with the five of us living in a two-bedroom house. Add in a few pups underfoot, and we'll be murdering each other for population control.

Return to the Pack

Chapter Eleven

Axel

After Callan and Luna eat, the triplets go to the garage to fiddle with their bikes, leaving Luna and me in the kitchen. I've got something to say to Luna but damned if I can't seem to get the words out.

While she does dishes, I head to the fridge to grab a beer. Before I get there, I wrap my arms around her from behind and draw her into my chest.

"Mmm," she says, leaning into me while water drips from her glove-covered hands. She's taken the wearing gloves to clean dishes because that's what Callan does. The only reason Callan does it is to keep the motorcycle grime and grease from smearing all over the dishes, but none of us are going to complain about Luna keeping her hands soft.

She's so damn innocent, I get a surge of protectiveness inside just thinking of her.

I kiss her neck and release her, heading for the fridge. I grab a cold one, twist off the top, and step back to my seat at the kitchen table.

"Want help?" I ask before sitting.

"You could dry the dishes," she offers sweetly.

"Sure thing." I bolt to my feet. We all treat Luna like royalty now that we've all done our part to hopefully produce an heir. "Where are the towels?"

She lets out a giggle as she stacks a pan in the dish rack. "You don't know where the kitchen towels are?"

"Why would I?" I start pulling out drawers, finding nothing but cutlery, dishes, bowls, and other kitchen stuff.

"We've lived here long enough for you to know where the towels are."

"That would imply that I've helped with the dishes," I say with a smirk. "That's your and Callan's thing."

"Ethan helps sometimes." She scrubs at the pan used to cook the meat. "There are five of us now. It's a big job."

"Warrick and I don't do the domestic duties." I pull out another drawer and find a stack of fluffy white towels. "We assume other responsibilities, like making sure you're safe and bred."

I step behind her and bite the side of her neck gently, wrapping my arms around her and resting my palms over her belly.

She places the last plate in the rack and leans back into me with a sigh of pleasure.

"To be continued," I murmur against her sweet skin before stepping away and getting busy drying the dishes.

"Why not now?" Her lips form an adorable pout.

"I've got to do the dishes," I say, reaching for a plate. "And you've got to put them away when I hand them to you."

A frown skitters across her face, but she grabs the plate I hand her, dries it, and dutifully places it on the shelf.

We work like that in silence as I muster up the courage for my question. Out of the corner of my eye, I glance out the window.

The three triplets are making their way back to the house.

It's now or never time. I pitch the towel on the counter and turn to her, taking her hands in mine and staring deep into her beautiful eyes. "Marry me, Luna."

"Marry you?" Her eyebrows raise high. "Okay, I guess."

"Do you know what it means to get married?" I ask, confused by her lack of enthusiasm.

The screen door bangs open.

"Married," she says thoughtfully, tapping her lips with her fingertips.

"What's this about marriage?" Warrick says, wiping his hands on a shop rag as he strides into the kitchen.

Callan and Ethan trail behind him. "Who's getting married?"

"Axel and I are!" Luna says brightly.

"What the fuck?" Warrick says, coming up to me and shoving me backward.

"Hey," I shout and shove him back.

"Real smooth waiting for us to be gone before you made your move with Luna," Warrick growls. He hauls back his arm as if to slug me.

"Stop!" Luna cries, seizing Warrick's arm. "No more fighting, remember? We can all get married if you tell me what marriage is."

"Don't be ridiculous," Ethan snarls, approaching Axel with rage in his eyes. "Marriage is a commitment between two people. Axel was hoping to separate you from us."

Luna sidles between us and extends her arms between my chest and Ethan's. "I said *no fighting!* You all agreed to share, so we'll share. Let's all get married."

Warrick, Ethan, Callan, and I eye one another uneasily.

"It's never been done," Warrick says, shooting daggers into my eyes.

"I don't care if it's never been done," Luna says. "That's what you said about us all being mates with me, too. Did that stop us?" She folds her arms across her chest, and damn if she isn't the most adorable spitfire of a woman who ever existed.

My gaze is still locked with Warrick's. Using our pack bond, I telepathically communicate with him. *She's right. The pack accepted it. The world will just have to deal with it, too.*

His bushy eyebrows launch high on his forehead as if he's unused to such subtle communication.

A light, bright silvery voice cuts into our stare-down.

"I love you," Luna says, her eyes pleading. "I love all of y'all. No one more than anyone else." A pretty smile spreads across her face, and she studies us each in turn, as if to get our reassurance that we all love her, too.

"About this marriage business..." Warrick says, still appearing to simmer.

"I'm so in love with this woman I can't and won't exist without her," I say flatly. I'm not one who does big emotions easily, but for Luna, it's worth it. "I didn't intend to separate her from the rest of you. I only meant to secure our commitment with a proposal. It didn't cross my mind to ask permission because I wasn't doing anything wrong. If she's having a baby, one of us should make an honest woman out of her, and it makes most sense for it to be me. I'm the Alpha, and being the Alpha's wife gives her most status and protection. She can have as many mates as she wants."

Luna scoffs. "While I do love each and every one of you, I think I'm at my limit. Four lovers are plenty."

Laughter breaks out among us, easing the tension.

"Still," I say. "Someone's gotta marry her, and it might cause some disturbance in the pack if we all tried to claim her as a wife. I mean…Luna and her four husbands?"

Shaking his head, Ethan pulls out a longneck for himself, then looks to his brothers.

Warrick and Callan lift their chins in assent.

Ethan tosses each a bottle of beer.

They catch them and twists the tops off. Foam bubbles out of the top, shooting all over their hands as they swig their beverages.

Callan pulls out a kitchen chair and settles into it, and the rest of us follow suit.

"It's up to Luna," Callan says. "If she wants four men, she gets four men, as long it's us four."

"I agree," Ethan says, resting his bottle on the kitchen table. "We've all fucked tons of women and didn't worry about public opinion even when we shared or passed them around, club whores and shit. Why should we worry about it now? Anyone who wants to give her shit can come talk to us."

I don't like him comparing my precious mate to a motorcycle club whore, but Luna doesn't seem to notice. She picks up a tortilla chip from the half-empty bowl on the table and nibbles at it. "What does this marriage business entail? Why do I need to do it for a baby?"

"It's a sacred bond between a woman and a man," I say. "Someone officiates the ceremony and others bear witness—typically the pack, in our case."

"Would that official person be Elder Amexaryl?" Her nose wrinkles up.

"Are you okay with that? Because, if you're not...." I start, intending to let her know I'll grant her any wish, even if I have to travel far to find the right officiate.

She holds out her palm. "We can use her. We made peace at the ritual with the pack. I understand now that it wasn't her intention to harm me in any way. She was merely performing her role within the pack."

Newfound wisdom and radiance emanate from Luna and, as I regard her, I feel myself falling deeper in love with her, as I do each day. "Are you sure?" I ask, reaching for her hand.

"I'm positive." She takes my hand and laces her fingers in mine.

"I think you might be right about one thing. There might be pushback from the pack," Ethan says before glugging down some beer.

"Tough shit," Warrick says. "When have we ever given a shit about gossip? We rule the pack. We can do whatever we want."

"Especially you," Callan says to his brother.

Warrick nods his shaggy head. "I'd just as soon pick my teeth with the bones of the gossipers than let them spoil my mood about a decision made in the privacy of our own home. If our baby girl wants her pussy pounded by four rough bikers every night, that's her business and our business and no one else's."

Though I'm not as rough as these outlaws and wouldn't phrase it quite that way myself, the sentiment he just tossed out into the room feels right. As I sit in this kitchen, cramped with the triplets and Luna, I can't help but settle comfortably into the rightness of the five of us together. I never in a million years thought I'd share my mate with three other men. Hell, less than six months ago, I never even thought I'd *have* a mate, and I sure as fuck wouldn't have let these assholes touch her.

But if Luna wants to marry us all, I'm not going to stand in her way. The only thing I care about is being with her, now and forever. No one's going to snatch her away from me—not these rebels, and not any roving, mutant lone wolves. We're bound together as mates, and soon we'll be bound by marriage. If she's bound to three other men, that doesn't make our connection any less real. If that's what makes her happy, I'll buy their fucking rings myself.

Anything for my Luna.

Chapter Twelve

Luna

Five people living in a house meant for two men is tight. Even before I moved in, Callan and Ethan had to take turns using their room or a mattress on the floor. We all feel crowded, and at times it gets to us, no matter how much we love each other. We each have to wait our turn to use the bathroom.

I like to take a bath, sometimes by myself. But my four men also need showers, and there's never enough hot water to go around. Just last night, Warrick came in from the garage. He'd been working on his motorcycle, so he got to use the shower as soon as I was done with my bath. Axel said that *he* should get the shower before Warrick since he's the Alpha.

That didn't go down well with Warrick.

When things like that come up, tempers flare. I make sure to ease the tension in bed with plenty of pleasure for all, but I can't help thinking Callan's right. We need a bigger house if we're going to be adding more people to it, even tiny people.

Return to the Pack

On the bright side, the closeness has brought us, well, closer. We don't just fuck anymore. Axel says what we do is called "making love." All I know is that it's a rich experience I have no words for. I don't care what it's called—mating or fucking or making love. It's all amazing.

This morning I woke up surrounded by three big bodies, some of them snoring. Warrick always exits to his own room, saying he needs room to spread out.

I can't help but smile—I love these guys. And today, Axel and I will see Elder Amexaryl set the marriage ritual, whatever that entails, in play.

I extricate myself from the pile and head to the kitchen to make breakfast.

After breakfast and cleanup, Axel and I make our way to his truck, hand in hand. He seems especially happy as he opens the passenger door for me.

"You've got a bright smile on your face today," I say, hopping into the cab.

He leans forward and kisses me. When he withdraws, he says, "How can I not be with you by my side?"

Then, he closes the door and rounds the bumper to his side of the truck. We travel in the truck to find Elder Amexaryl's place. It's situated as deep in the swamp as I used to live, though it's outside Bogbeast Waters and still in wolf territory. It's in an isolated and remote region, with only the alligators for companionship.

Axel parks the truck in a clearing surrounded by Tupelo trees. Some of the leggy trees rest in swamp water. Lily pads and bright green duck grass float in the water. The watchful, unblinking eyes of a couple of alligators track our movement. We pick our way through the bog to find a house on stilts with a deck right at the edge of the swamp water.

Elder Amexaryl sits outside with her slender legs dangling in the water. When she sees us, she climbs to her feet with the grace of an antelope, surprisingly agile for one so old. Her colorful dress settles around her ankles, and she waves, calling, "Go around to the back of the house. I'll meet you there."

We nod and head to the door facing the forest. Painted gourds and plants in terra cotta pots line the wooden walkway to her house. Lizards skitter out of the way, disturbed from their late morning slumber. At the front door, creepy-looking gray sculpted creatures hang menacingly from the corners. Water drips down their sides like they've taken a dip in the swamp.

"Those are my gargoyles," Axel says when I shudder. "They scare off evil and channel rainwater out of their open mouths."

"They're not real, are they?"

"Don't think so," Axel says, peering through a small circular hole cut in the door.

Return to the Pack

One of the creatures turns his head to look at the other.

"Axel," I say, tugging on his arm.

"What?" he says, looking down at me, but he's interrupted as the door swings wide.

Elder Amexaryl smiles at us and opens the door. She seems much more relaxed in her home environment than she does when she's on duty, performing her job. "Come in, come in," she says, pushing on the screen door.

When Axel steps into her home, one of the gargoyles leaps onto the floor.

I let out a yelp.

Axel tenses and whips around, jumping in front of me protectively.

"Rex!" Elder Amexaryl scolds. "Stop scaring my guests."

The creature leaps back into position on his corner of the door.

"Those two are Rex and Ralph, my pet gargoyles," Elder Amexaryl says. "They're actually shifters who live in these swamp waters. But for a regular meal, they can be coerced into doing the role they were born to do." She wags her finger at them. "You be nice to pack members— you know the difference between pack members and unwelcome intruders. Shame on you." She turns and leads us into her cozy, colorful dwelling.

Axel and I stand near the worn couch until she gestures for us to sit, and then we take our seats.

"I hear you need my assistance again," she says, settling into a rocking chair. She begins to rock in a slow, hypnotic rhythm, causing the floor and the chair to creak.

"Yes," Axel says, leaning forward. "I'd like to marry Luna."

I clear my throat and cast a look his way.

"Actually," he corrects himself. "Callan, Ethan, Warrick, and I would like to marry Luna."

"I see," Elder Amexaryl says, continuing to rock. "This is a most unusual request."

"It may be unusual, but it feels so right," I blurt, afraid she'll deny us our request. "I love them all. I can't imagine life without any of them. I can't choose!"

Elder Amexaryl nods, leveling me with her pale gaze. Then she turns to Axel. "And you're content with this, Alpha?"

"Yes. Luna is my heart. I learned by my foolish actions that it stops beating if she's not a part of my world."

I give him a side-eye and reach for his hand. "Can Axel and I...can our True Mate bond be restored, also? I think it still exists. I'm sure I ran away before the bond was completely severed. That's why we still love each other."

Axel gives me a look of love that makes my wolf feel like warm, liquid sunshine. But there's pain behind that gaze like he still carries the shame of severing our bond.

I turn to Elder Amexaryl. "I still feel the bond. I know it's there. Our True Mate bond lives in each of our hearts."

Elder Amexaryl studies me, compassion radiating from her gaze. Then, she shakes her head. "No, child... I'm sorry. The True Mate bond was truly severed."

I shake my head. "It can't be. We, Axel and I... We weren't ready to accept it, but it still exists, I know it does." I take Axel's hand. "We are bound, and nothing can sever that. Even when we were apart, we ached for each other."

Elder Amexaryl pats the air in front of her. "Be still, child. No need to get agitated. I can't change the past or the truth. You and Axel are mates. But the magical bond we severed through ritual is gone. *Nothing* can destroy your love, though. That is a choice you can make every day. The connection you share goes deeper than fate. It's in your heart."

I scoot closer to Axel, and he puts his arm around me, pulling me close. I'm *so* happy to hear her say this that I could cry.

"Your mother and father were True Mates." Elder Amexaryl stares as if she's looking into the beyond. "Your father was a good man. It broke your mother to lose him."

"I know," I say, a bitter smile forming on my face. "I lived with Mama's broken self. As soon as I came of age, I cared for her as *her* mother. Now that I've felt the bond severed, I know how it could destroy a person."

"But you're stronger than her," Axel murmurs.

"I never knew what it was like to be cared for until joining the triplets."

Elder Amexaryl reins in her gaze, returning from wherever she traveled in her mind. "You have suffered great tragedies, Luna."

Curiosity bubbles in me, filling my head with questions. "Were you there? When my father died, I mean?"

She nods her head, causing her whitish hair to swirl. "Such a tragedy."

"I never understood it," Axel says. "How could the entire pack turn on one of our own?"

"Is that what you heard?" One of Elder Amexaryl's eyebrows rises high on her forehead. "I could use some refreshments. How about you?"

Her odd invitation in the middle of a conversation gives me pause. I glance at Axel, who mirrors my perplexed stare.

"Water, I guess, sure," I say.

"Sure. Some water would be great," Axel agrees.

When Elder Amexaryl disappears into her tiny kitchen, Axel and I look at one another.

"That was abrupt," he says.

"I wonder what she doesn't want to tell us?" I say, a frown creasing my forehead.

Elder Amexaryl returns bearing three glasses of water with herbs floating in each one. "Here you go," she says, handing one to each of us.

We each sip our drinks, waiting for her to explain.

She finishes the entire glass before speaking. "Your father wasn't killed by the pack. He was murdered by maneater wolves, the kind of which is hunting you."

Shock pins me to my seat. "Maneater wolves murdered my father?"

"That's right," she says. "Your father fought valiantly, but the mutant wolves were too strong. The pack rallied together to beat back maneaters, eventually chasing them off. We haven't heard of them for years. Until now."

Chapter Thirteen

Luna

Elder Amexaryl's words slam into my belly like a missile. I can't believe it. All those years living alone with my mother, taking care of her, dodging her attempts at my life when the voices in her head took over, all her rants about not trusting the pack, not trusting wolves... It was all a lie. She poisoned my mind against being able to trust a living soul, when the truth was, it wasn't the pack at all. It was maneater wolves who killed my father.

And the same aberrant mutant wolves that are hunting me, murdered my father.

Why would she deny me a life with the pack? How dare she ruin my life this way? Was it just her addled mind mixing up mutant wolves with the pack? Or generalizing the danger and in her paranoia believing all wolves were dangerous?

Elder Amexaryl looks at me, concern creasing the corners of her eyes. "I'm sorry, child."

"Did she know it was one of those mutants who took my father's life?" I say, sure my skin has drained of color.

"Yes," the elder says, nodding. "She knew."

My limbs begin to tremble as it sinks in. The walls seem to shrink, and suddenly, my clothes, this house, everything seems too tight. I bolt to my feet and race for the door, my wolf bursting forth.

"Luna! Wait! What's going on?" Axel calls.

I let out a howl, shoving open the screen door and bursting out in my wolf skin.

Rex and Ralph leap from their positions in the corners of the door and scamper away.

I charge down the dirt driveway, heading for the woods, for somewhere I can clear my mind.

"Leave her be," Elder Amexaryl says from what sounds like far behind me. "She needs time to process."

"But…" Axel protests.

"No, Alpha. Don't follow her," Elder Amexaryl says in that voice of hers that could make you slit your own throat, the one even an Alpha must obey.

Shifting, I run as fast and as far as my legs will carry me. I propel my body beneath branches and over stumps. I swim through ponds and streams, heedless of my surroundings.

Once I come to a stop, I throw back my head and howl. "How could you do this to me, Mama? How could you keep me all to yourself? You knew the entire time it wasn't the pack who betrayed you. It was the same bastards who are hunting me now." I fall to my knees as sobs break through the rage. I feel betrayed by my mother and by the entire pack. Most of them must have been alive to tell the tale when I emerged from the woods and entered their world.

The stillness of the woods seems to cradle me in its arms, rocking me. I curl into a ball the same way I used to curl in our ramshackle shack, feeling alone and too young to care for my mother. Eyes squeezed shut, I listen to the birds fluttering about in the trees. Insects crawl across my skin, tickling me. But being alone like this, the way I lived every day of my life out in Bogbeast Waters, now feels foreign. I have people who care about me now. Axel, Ethan, Callan, Warrick—even members of the pack care for me. Despite my mother's foolishness, I've come to know and appreciate pack life. I know what it's like to be part of a loving family.

The soft pad of wolf feet pricks at my ears. *Is it one of those murdering wolves?* I scramble out of my curled-up position and set my senses to high alert.

But the wolf who emerges from the trees is a welcome one—Axel, come to comfort me.

Tail wagging, he trots across the leaf-strewn forest floor to me and licks my face, my ears, my neck, my muzzle. I roll over, presenting my belly to my Alpha.

Return to the Pack

Three more wolves pad through the underbrush, and I wriggle to my feet and trot towards them. It's my pack—Callan, Ethan, and Warrick, joining Axel in consoling me.

Once we've loved one another in that joyous manner that wolves share. When they're done, we all shift back into human form.

"That pack bond let us know Luna was in distress," Callan says. "The others heard it, too, so we took off as fast as we could to find you."

"Your call came through as clear as a bell," Warrick states, grinning at me.

"Being in a pack is beneficial to all wolves," Axel says from his position by my side. "Lone wolves too often get into trouble—like these maneaters."

"So, what it is, Luna? What's causing you so much grief?" Ethan says, smoothing my hair away from my face.

"It's my mother," I say, my lip trembling a little. "She lied to me all these years about who murdered my father."

"How so?" Callan asks.

"Those horrible freak wolves killed him, not pack members," I say.

"Whoa," Callan says. "Seriously?"

"It's true." Axel nods his head. "Elder Amexaryl just told us."

"Why would she think to tell us now? Why didn't she say something before?" Warrick says, scratching his scruffy beard.

Axel shrugs. "The pack apparently beat the maneaters back. Maybe she hoped it wasn't true—that they're back."

"I feel so betrayed," I say, scooting closer to Callan. Leaves and sticks are digging into my rump. Being a wolf in the woods is so much easier than being a human with our too-soft skin.

Callan lifts me onto his lap. "You can't change what's passed, Luna. You know that. She made a mistake. We all make mistakes. She's no longer around to make amends—that's the bitch part about death. You'd better hope you make your peace before you cross over because you might not get another chance." He leans over and kisses my cheek.

"Is there anything good you can remember about your mother?" Ethan asks.

"No," I say, without thinking twice.

"Nothing?" Warrick says, sitting directly across from me. "I mean, we can relate to not having the best stories to tell about our upbringing, but I can remember a time when Mom and Dad took us hunting. We were all pups. It might have been our first hunting lesson as a family. And you, Ethan, your legs wouldn't cooperate with your body, and you kept stumbling. You fell over logs, rocks, everything… Dad kept pulling you to your feet by the scruff of your neck." Laughing, he points at his brother.

"Did not," Ethan says with a scowl.

"Yeah, you did," Callan says, joining Warrick in the slide down memory lane. "And then you got obsessed with your tail and chased it around and around. Been chasing tail ever since."

"Hey," Ethan protests.

Callan laughs. "Warrick and I just sat and waited for you to finish. Finally, Mom grabbed you by the neck and shook you to your senses."

Warrick grins. "We didn't catch anything that day, but we sure had fun."

Ethan reins in his raucous laughter and wipes his eyes, looking at me. "See? If we three can find something pleasant in that shitstorm of an upbringing, you can too, pup."

A sunbeam pokes its way through the branches and warms my head. I scratch at the dirt with my fingernails, thinking of the past. "I remember after a hurricane, when the waterways were filled with crap, people's belongings and whatnot, Mama took me on a collecting trip. The goal was to find useful things for our house. We found a watersoaked loveseat floating in the swamp and dragged it out of the water and let it dry in the sun for a few days before hauling it home." I wrinkle up my nose. "It always smelled funny, but it was a comfy place to sit and eat sometimes. We had fun that day."

Callan smiles and squeezes me to him, rubbing his beard against my shoulder.

Another memory pops to the surface. "Oh! And there's the time we chased dragonflies through the meadow. The dragonflies would land on my back or my head and hang tight. Mom would race over and snap at them, but they were too fast. They just flew into the air and took off. That was one of Mama's good days. She didn't have the moods that day."

Sudden sadness drips over my fleeting good memories. "The good days were seldom. Mama was a mess inside. She often fell into nightmares, screaming and thrashing about how evil wolves were and crying to protect me from them. 'You can't take my Luna!' she'd scream. 'You can't have her.'"

Callan strokes my back, now warm from the sunshine. "Maybe she got the mutant wolves all mixed up in her mind with the rest of the pack, and she was trying to protect you from them. Her mind must have warped over losing her True Mate."

I glance over at Axel, whose face is stony though his eyes are deep with sadness. He and I—we went nuts when our True Mate bond was broken. I could have ended up like Mama. Maybe I would have if I hadn't found these men to save me from that fate and love me back to life.

"Don't you go there, you two," Callan says, his gaze shifting between Axel and me. "You grew from that moment. We all did." With a somber gaze, he lets his attention drift to his brothers and then to Axel. "We're a family now. We're a pack. No one's letting Luna run off in the swamp with that pup in her belly."

"Never?" I ask, my voice small.

He gives me such a warm gaze my chest fills with joy. "I love you, Luna. I love you like I've never loved before. I don't think I've ever loved a woman before… Not even close. Not if I compare it with what I feel for you."

Emotion clogs up my throat. "I love you, too." I let my gaze linger on his beautiful eyes before turning to face Warrick. "And you…I love you, Warrick."

Warrick clears his throat and nods.

"And, you, Ethan. My heart is full of love for you."

Ethan blinks rapidly and nods. "I love you, too, Luna. You know that," he says gruffly.

"And you, Axel," I say. "You're right. We've searched for one another through time. We just didn't know we needed to find these guys, too." My heart is bursting right now with all the love I feel for my mates.

"You'll turn us into saps, girl," Warrick says in his gravelly voice.

"Pups like you," Ethan chokes out.

I laugh, unable to hold back my emotion. "Speaking of pups, I want our puppies—our kids—to grow up happy and free, without fear. Our children should be raised in the warmth of the pack with lots of playmates. Promise me, y'all. Promise me we'll make that happen. Let's not let what happened to me or to you three with your mean dad… Let's not let that happen to our own children."

Callan gets to his feet and places me on mine. The others rise, too.

Warrick pounds his fist against his palm. "We've got to hunt ourselves some motherfucking mutants and send them into the ground. Then, and only then, will I consider you and our pups safe, Luna."

That's when I realize where they all found me just now—running blindly, without reason, I made my way back home, to the swamp just outside the triplet's house.

Chapter Fourteen

Axel

I need some space from our cramped living conditions, so I head to Creebay Preserve to meet with the vampires the following evening. For weeks now, I've been torn between my pack responsibilities and that of my heart. First, dealing with my own stupidity over severing my True Mate bond took its toll on me. Then, trying to atone for my mistakes and fix what I'd destroyed captured all of my attention. The hurricane distracted us all. And then, when Luna went into heat—well, I don't need to mention what direction my drive went during that fan-fucking-tastic week.

These thoughts nearly send me back into the house for more of my Luna, but I think she's busy with Callan right now, so I wrench my mind back on today's task and climb into the truck.

It's a beautiful day in Florida today, transforming into a perfect evening. The sun is dipping toward the horizon, painting rippling clouds in shades of red and fiery orange, and the temperature hangs in the mid-eighties. I hope to get back in time for a turn with Luna in the sultry still of the night.

With the window open wide and my arm resting on the frame, I accelerate and zip away from the triplet's home, heading for pack land.

Half an hour later, I park near the clearing, exit the truck, and forge my way through the woods to the land I gifted the vampires.

As I pass the area on which we should be building a home for Luna, my belly tightens. I'm still pissed at myself for giving that piece of property in particular to the vampires. But what can I say? I was desperate to get her back. I'd have given anything, and I did—I gave away the place we could have built the perfect place to raise our children and live comfortably with the triplets.

"You can't change the past," I grumble under my breath as I trek across the damp earth.

In the distance, I spy a building in construction. When I get closer, I pause, taking in the grandeur of what will soon be the vampire's chief domain. It looks like a sweeping three-story mansion will quickly occupy this section of the preserve.

A strangled growl leaves my throat. "What an idiot," I mutter. "I could have done better than to give them all this land." Huffing out a lungful of breath, I stride in the direction of the three small cabins they presumably occupy.

A whoosh sounds and two vampires blur before me, blocking my path.

"This land is private," Drake says as his body becomes opaque.

"As in, *you* can't enter," Evan says, stabbing my chest with his finger.

I shove away his hand, wincing at the jab that's certain to leave a bruise. "I come in peace. I have news for you."

"What kind of news?" Drake says. "Have you found our feeding stations?"

"No," I say. "Is there somewhere we can sit down and do this in a civilized manner?"

Drake and Evan eye one another. I know tapping into the vampires need to appear the most sophisticated of the supernaturals will get me where I need to go. They think we're a bunch of hot-headed animals, and they're not wrong, but wolves have brains, too..

Drake gives a subtle lift of his chin to Even, giving him the go-ahead to speak.

"Those wolves attacked again last night," Evan says. "They ransacked my house, so my dwelling isn't up to the standard we're used to. We wouldn't dream of seeing guests in the shambles that remain."

"They attacked again?" I demand, the hairs on my head, neck, and arms prickling in alarm.

"Yes," Drake says. "And since you gave us your word, it isn't you, we haven't yet destroyed any pack members."

"We wanted to," Evan says, puffing out his chest.

"Evan," Drake says in a low, menacing voice. "We spoke of this." He places his hand on Evan's shoulder, and Evan's stance softens slightly.

"I know with certainty who's responsible—it's those mutant wolves I told you about," I say, matching Evan's puffed-up stance. No one's going to bow up on me and intimidate me.

"So, what are you going to do about it?" Drake says in a heart-chilling voice.

"What am *I* going to do about it? I'm doing all I can," I say, throwing out my arms. "They're not a part of my pack. What are *you* going to do about it? You should be able to destroy them without pack assistance. You certainly have no qualms about attacking *my* wolves."

Evan looks down and shifts side to side. "We've tried."

Drake's nostrils flare.

"What happens when you try?" I ask, crossing my arms over my chest and narrowing my eyes.

"Those fucking wolves are monsters," Drake says. "They're impossibly strong and sneaky, too, for a beast so oversized. Somehow they managed to sneak up on us twice now."

"Don't you leave guards to watch?" I ask.

"We're not used to having to resort to such fearful tactics," Drake says, looking down his nose at me.

"And we need our repose," Evan says.

"Ah," I say, nodding. Vampires don't do well in daylight, after all. Wolves prefer to hunt at night, too, but we don't have to. And we certainly defend our land at all hours. "Well, you might start resorting to such *fearful tactics*. You might find them useful if you frame it differently in your mind. Like, *these giant, dangerous maneating animals are roaming the woods, murdering everything in their path for reasons unknown, and we need to be watchful.*"

"Don't push me, mutt," Drake threatens.

"Pushing? What I'm doing is *warning* you. Giving you a heads up to let you know what we're all dealing with." My fingers coil, taut and ready. Vampires and wolves are always at each other's throats.

"Thanks a lot," Evan mutters. "We might thank you more if you controlled your kind."

I rein in my frustration. "Look, these fuckers are our *enemies*. They're not our kind—they've mutated from eating human flesh. And they're your enemies as well as mine. At the very least, we could do everything in our power to stop them, if not by joining forces, then separately."

Drake gives me a chilly gaze. "We'll take your words under advisement." He offers a subtle tilt of his head in Evan's direction, and they fade from view.

"Vampires," I mutter, rolling my eyes. Then, I turn to head out of their goddamned territory inside *my pack's* preserve.

I love the feel of the night as it blankets me with its soothing darkness. All my senses grow acute. In human form, they're still dumbed down, so I shift into a wolf. This way, I can smell everything, see sharper, hear the drop of a mouse whisker twenty yards away. As I lope toward my truck, I detour through the woods that line the swamp. I wish Luna was with me. I'm going to have to bring her hunting with me again. In fact, the thought of a family hunt gets my blood pumping. That would bond us outside the bedroom as much as sharing Luna during her heat did inside it.

Ahead, a small vole has grown still, sensing my presence. I loom over it, barely breathing. Then, I rear up on my hind legs and pounce.

He's too quick for me and pops into his burrow, away from my waiting mouth. I let out a sneeze of laughter and forge deeper into the preserve.

Ahead, wolf growls ring out, so I stop and sniff the air. It's pack members, so I trot towards them. When we're in visual range, we all shift into our human forms so we can talk.

Return to the Pack

"Hey, Axel," Kato says, standing next to Borris, Adopha, Chann, Hati, and Lobo.

A sliver of a moon lights the sky behind him.

"Out for a hunt?" I ask.

"Hell, yes," Borris says. "We've all been too focused on repairs after the storm. It's such an awesome night we thought to head on out and have some fun. You?"

"Same. Well, I had to deliver the news to the vamps that the mutant wolves are definitely the culprits. They attacked their lair again last night."

"No one on guard after the last attack?" Kato says.

"What a bunch of idiots," Chann says, shaking his head.

"That's what I said. They may be cavalier about the whole affair, but we need to prepare for war."

"Yeah," Kato says, glancing at Borris. "Warrick already told us."

"What? When did he do that?" I try not to react, but my blood's boiling. He's supposed to run all his plans through me. He's my Second, not the pack Alpha.

"Um," Kato says, appearing uncomfortable. "When was it, y'all?"

"This afternoon," Hati says. He looks as uncomfortable as Kato. "When he brought the weapons."

I can't appear unsure to my pack, so I snap my fingers and say, "Oh, right, I did tell him to drop those by. Too much shit on my mind."

I shake my head, and Kato slaps my back. "I hear you. Life's crazy anymore, right?"

"It sure is."

Everyone grins and relaxes out of their moment of discomfort.

"I'd better get back home," I say. "Dinner's waiting."

"Yes, Alpha," Borris says, lifting his hand in farewell.

"Later," Kato says. Before he shifts and gets back into hunting mode, he says, "Tell Warrick if he finds any more weapons, we'll put them to good use."

"Will do," I manage to choke out. I turn and stride toward my truck, fuming. Once I start it up, I speed back to the triplets at a breakneck speed.

I skid to a stop in the driveway, throw open the door, and leap from my vehicle.

The garage is lit up, so I head there, sure that Warrick is out there messing with his ride.

Sure enough, he's sitting on an ancient plastic milk cart from years back. "Hey," he grunts when I enter the room, not taking his eyes off the engine. He grips the wrench in his hand and twists a bolt.

"Remember how you gave me shit for asking for Luna's hand in marriage without consulting with the rest of you?" I demand.

His eyebrows stitch together, but his gaze stays glued to whatever task he's performing. "Yeah? What about it?"

"What the fuck are you doing going to the pack without consulting me?" I shout. "It's *my* pack. You're my *Second*. You don't talk to them about going to war with the lone wolves or give them our fucking weapons. That's my job, Warrick."

"What the fuck is your problem?" He stands and takes two steps toward me, towering over me. "You've been kind of busy, Romeo, so I thought I was doing you a favor." He grabs the neck of my t-shirt, twisting it in his grasp.

"You're overstepping," I growl at him. "If you want to challenge me for Alpha, be a man and fucking do it. Don't sneak around behind my back like a pathetic little pussy."

Warrick yanks the t-shirt in his hold, jerking me off-balance. "Is that what you think I'm doing?"

Warrick is a threatening presence on his best days. But when he's mad, red-faced, eyes bulging, looking at me like he could eat me for dinner, he's looks like death itself. Fighting to the death is standard when an Alpha is challenged, though. My whole life is a balancing act, and nothing is guaranteed. One day, someone will take my place. It could be today or tomorrow or in twenty years.

"Isn't it?" I snap back at the meathead.

"I opened my home to you, asshole. Why would I want to slide in and take over the pack?" His spit sprays my face, but I make no move to wipe it off. "I've got enough on my plate being your Second, joining the pack, fucking our mate senseless every night, and making sure my brothers don't murder anyone in your pack. I'm not trying to take over."

"All directives come through *me*." I pound my chest with my fist.

"I'm your *Second*," he says, glowering. "I've been informed by my prick of an Alpha that decisions can be made when said Alpha is otherwise engaged. And you've been otherwise engaged." He releases his hold on my shirt and slaps his palm against my chest.

It stings, but I don't react.

"Christ, just a few weeks ago, we all thought you were dead. Would I have cared? Not for myself. After we brought you here, did I *want* you to move in? Fuck, no. Did I set aside my preferences and do it anyway? Yes, I did. I did it for Luna. Because I love her, and for some fucking reason, she loves you." His shouting makes the walls of the garage shake.

We stare at one another, unwilling to show weakness and look away first.

Luna races through the garage door, and we look away at the same time. "What's going on?" she cries. "I thought something happened to you, Warrick."

"Something did happen to me," Warrick says in a quieter voice. "Your boy here got in my grill about 'going behind his back' and speaking to the pack today about matters which concern us all."

"Axel," she says, and my name lands like a punch to the gut.

"What?" I snap. "He went over my head, making me look like an asshole in front of the pack."

"He wanted to take some of the burdens off your shoulders," she says in a voice like honey. "He told me before he left today."

Now I feel like a bigger idiot, but I'm not going to let Luna see that, and I'm definitely not going to let Warrick see.

She turns to Warrick and says, "And I thought when you told me you'd already cleared it with Axel."

"No," Warrick says, scowling. "I'm not used to checking in with people to get shit done." He crosses his arms over his massive chest and glares at me.

"And I'm not used to people performing my role in the pack," I say, matching his stance.

"I did it to *help* you, Axel," Warrick says, his voice calmer.

"Thank you," I grit out. "But I shouldn't be hearing it after the fact."

"Yeah, okay," he acknowledges.

"He did open his home to you, Axel," Luna says. "Otherwise, you'd be sleeping on someone's couch."

Yes, I think glumly. *Without you by my side.*

This whole situation is kind of fucked. With all the dominant energy in the house, it's a good thing we have Luna's calming presence or we'd have ripped each other to shreds by now. Clearly, we need some space. We're living on top of one another. And so, I hold out my hand to Warrick to shake.

He pumps my hand. "We good?" he asks, slapping me on the back with his free hand.

"Yeah, we're good. As long as you understand you can't undermine me to the pack like that."

"Yeah," he grunts, and I know he'll never apologize, but that's all right. "Won't happen again."

I wouldn't expect it from a dominant wolf like him. He'll learn his place and get used to it, and allowing for that is part of my job as Alpha, just as I'd allow any submissive to make mistakes. That's part of pack life, and part of family life, too.

Chapter Fifteen

Luna

Living with four men has its challenges—just as we get one conflict squared away between Axel and Warrick when Axel asked me to marry him, the next one flares up like a forest fire. Last night it sounded like two ogres bellowing in the garage when in fact it was only Warrick and Axel at each other's throats again. But now, Axel and Warrick are playing horseshoes in the front yard while I lounge nearby in the warm sun.

Where, oh, where are we going to find our next home?

"Luna!" Callan's voice comes from inside the house.

"Out here," I shout. I want to slip deep into the woods for some peace and quiet, but with rogue wolves on the loose, I'm not allowed to be alone.

The screen door slaps open, and Callan bounces from the house, grinning broadly. He makes his way over to me and settles next to me in an old metal chair left out here to rust. "I've got all the food planned for our wedding.

It's going to be a feast. Venison over the fire-pit, potato salad, apple pie, the works…"

"Oh?" I say, not knowing why all this fuss has to be made for a wedding. I've been so busy trying to keep peace in the house it slipped my mind to ask what a wedding entails. "So, there's a ceremony *and* a dinner? Seems like a lot of work."

"No, silly pup," he says, rising from the rusty chair and sinking onto the ground beside me and kneading them into my shoulders.

The feel of the warm air against my face, coupled with his warm hands, eases me out of my sour mood.

"I'm one of the grooms. I called Adolpha, and she and some of the other women are seeing to the food. She and I planned the feast." His hands move down my body, and tingles of pleasure coil between my thighs. Still, I'm unsure how I feel that he's called Adolpha and chatted with her extensively to plan this event.

"Luna," he says with a scoff.

"What?" I say.

"Don't be jealous." He flips over on top of me, holding himself a few inches off my body.

"Who says I'm jealous?"

He lowers himself and kisses me. "We're all connected telepathically, remember?"

"Do I have anything to worry about?" I say, scrunching up my face.

He places his hands on my cheeks and pulls me into a kiss. It's tender and slow as he moves his head in slow circles, moaning into my mouth and making wetness seep into my underwear.

He withdraws and looks at me with lowered eyelids. "Does that feel like the kind of kiss a guy you should be worried about would give you?"

"No, but…" I stare up at him.

"But nothing. I'm in love with you, girl." He taps the end of my nose. "Only you."

Reassured, I relax, running my bare feet gently up his thighs before linking them behind his ass and pulling him against me.

"That's better," he says, moving his hips against mine to let me feel the impressive size of his hard cock against my center.

"I guess I need to know more about this wedding business," I breathe. "All I know is it's a ceremony that Elder Amexaryl will conduct and then we'll all be married. What will be different, though? We all love each other already."

"We all love *you*, Luna. My brothers are still my brothers, and we're learning to all get along with Axel and work together as a team. This wedding shindig is making our commitment to you formally acknowledged and witnessed by the pack and everyone outside it. And we're all committing to you as our only lover."

"You won't love anyone else?"

"Never," he says, rubbing his nose gently back and forth against mine. "Or fuck them."

My heart swells hearing this. "And I only need y'all to keep me happy."

"Good." He gives his hips another push, sending me soaring with pleasure. "Because if another guy tries to touch you, we'll tear his head off and hang it outside the house as a warning to anyone else who gets any ideas."

For a long beat, we stay silent as I picture that, and my heart swells with warmth at his protectiveness.

I reach down, sliding my hand along his hard length. "What do I need to do for this wedding?" I ask.

"You need to go shopping," he murmurs.

"What for?" I say, tugging my skirt up so he's resting against my underwear.

"Because you need to look pretty for this here wedding," Callan says with a grin, winding my lilac hair around his fingers. "Not that you don't look pretty all the time."

I bat my eyelashes at him, taking his cock into my hand and guiding it to my pussy. "What do I need to look pretty?"

"Oh, girl things. I don't know." Callan groans and strains to get his thick cock inside me when I pull my panties aside. His girth finally breaches my entrance and sinks into me. "The devil in hell, but you're tight," he breathes. "Your cunt smells so good I want to eat it and fuck it at the same time."

He pumps into me slow and sweet, and when I look up, Warrick and Axel have stopped playing and come to watch. I can see a pronounced ridge in both their jeans, and my walls clench around Callan with desire. He grunts and thrusts into me harder, gripping my ass so I won't slide across the ground as his hips slam into mine. I lean up on my elbows to watch what they're seeing—me holding aside my panties as his big, slick cock plunges deep into my shaved pussy with each pass.

The sight makes me come almost immediately, and Callan finishes up a minute later. Then he straightens my clothes and climbs to his feet, pulling me with him.

"I think it's my turn now," Axel says.

"I noticed them going at it first," Warrick argues.

"Oh, boy," I say. "This again."

"Get Warrick to take you shopping," Callan says with a wink, heading for the house.

"Good idea," I say, turning to the other men. "You and Axel need some time away from one another, or you'll start fighting again."

Axel and Warrick glance at each other.

"Would you take me shopping today?" I ask, placing my palms on his chest.

"Nah," he says, backing toward the house. He pulls me with him as he lowers into the edge of the porch, lifting me onto his knee. "Let's stay here and do other things."

"She does need new clothes for the wedding," Axel says. "It's in a few days."

"Then a definite no to that idea," Warrick says. "I can't pick a wedding dress. Take Axel, baby girl. Better yet, send Axel to pick it out for you, and we can head to the bedroom." He gently squeezes my breasts, rolling the nipples with his fingers through my t-shirt. "I want to feel that sweet cunt milking my cock like it did Callan's."

I wiggle my rump against the erection forming in his pants.

"Nope, not me," Axel says, striding up the steps. "I've got pack business to attend to this afternoon."

"Need your Second in Command to be with you?" Warrick says, eyeing my mouth.

"Not this time," Axel says. "I have to help put out some domestic squabbles."

"Fuck," Warrick says, turning and calling into the house. "What about you, Callan? You're better than me with girly shit."

"Nope," Callan says. "I've got to go buy some parts for my bike."

"You can buy parts and then get whatever shit Luna needs," Warrick says, massaging my breasts until I want to take him up on his idea to stay here and fuck.

"Why can't Warrick and I stay home? Who says I need a new dress?" I ask breathlessly.

Callan marches onto the porch and tugs me from Warrick's lap. "Because you do. It's part of the ritual. We'll be wearing tuxedos, so you're going to get glammed up, too."

"Ohhh," I say, laughing. "Because *you're* getting dressed up, I have to get dressed up, too."

"Exactly," Callan says. "Now, *go*."

I turn to Warrick, and he tries to look grumpy, but a slight smile tugs the corners of his mouth. "Let's go then," I say. "We can make it fun. Remember how much fun we had when you bought me all those things like tampons and clothes?"

"Don't remind me," he grumbles. "I still bear the scars from that outing."

With a grunt, he pushes to his feet and takes my hand. "Let's go before I change my mind."

Out on the open road, sitting on the back of Warrick's motorcycle, I feel elated. I love riding on Warrick's Harley.

Warrick drives like the badass he is—fast and hard. We cruise along the dirt road heading away from the house until we get to the paved roads. Then he opens up the throttle, and we take off.

I've got one arm wrapped around his midline and the other one keeping a firm grasp on his hair, so it doesn't pummel the shield of my helmet. I'd rather not wear a helmet, since none of them do, but they've made it clear that I have to wear one. So, to keep the peace, I let them put it on me each time. At least it prevents me from getting slapped in the face by whirling hair.

We get to Jacksonville's largest mall in record time, thanks to Warrick's refusal to adhere to speed limits. Ethan explained it like this. He knows if the cops pull him over, he'll mess up their faces with his fists or grease their pockets with fat cash. They never know which. So they turn a blind eye to his speeding, hoping for the latter but fearing the former.

The mall is the very one we went to where Warrick had to buy me tampons, shampoo, and such. But this time we head for a different store.

"This is the one you want, Luna," he says, directing me across the blazing hot parking lot toward a store called, *Your Special Day*.

"That's a strange name for a store," I say.

"Yeah, well, girls get all goofy about weddings. But thank fuck, you're not one of those kinds of girls, or we definitely wouldn't be here," he says, reaching for the front door.

Tiny bells tinkle against the frame as he holds it open for me to enter.

I sashay past him and enter a world of white everything—long white dresses, white lacy headdress-looking things, white shoes, and white purses with beads all over them. Instantly I want to turn around and leave. It's like the cleanness inside shines a bright light on how grubby we are.

"Why, hello," a crisp-sounding voice says to me from across the room.

I look up to find a woman who looks like she sat on a stick. Everything about her is rigid, from her tight blond hairdo to the rose-colored dress clinging to rolls of flesh to the pale pink shoes her feet are jammed into.

At least she brings some color to this environment, as bleached out as everything looks, like bones laid out in the sun until they're pure, moon-white.

"Someone needs to remove that stick from her ass," Warrick mutters.

I giggle. "I was just thinking that!"

"How can I help you?" the woman says, barely moving her lips as she speaks. She eyes Warrick fearfully like he might lunge for her at any moment.

Knowing Warrick, he might, just to get a rise out of her.

A wicked grin spreads across his face. "My girl and I are getting hitched. We're having a biker's wedding. Ever been to one?"

"Why no, I haven't." Miss Tight Ass sidles behind a rack of shimmering cream-colored dresses, probably to keep something solid between her and Warrick. "But I'm sure we can find just the right dress for the occasion."

She nervously fingers a cloud-colored satin number in front of her.

"It needs to have easy access to this place," he says, palming his crotch and grinning. "Me and the boys all take a turn with her as part of the ceremony. There's a good number of us in the club, so it's a long night of fun."

Miss Tight Ass backs away, her eyes on me. "Do you consent to such behavior, dear?"

"I don't mind when they take turns or all go at once," I admit. "Both are fun in different ways."

The woman looks like she'll faint. Warrick chuckles and pulls me in, palming my breast and squeezing.

"I'm not sure if we're the right place for you," Miss Tight Ass says.

I swear, even the skin on her face doesn't move when she talks.

"Really," says Warrick, pulling a fat roll of cash from his pocket. "That's a shame because I want her to look pretty. It ain't every day you get hitched, you know."

Miss Tight Ass's eyes glitter as she looks at the wad of green bills in Warrick's hand. "Maybe I can find you something," she says at last.

"But not white," I say with a frown. "These dresses are all too bright. The wedding guests will need sunglasses if I wear one of these."

The shopkeeper's lips form a tight sphincter.

"What about this one, doll?" Warrick says, lifting a short, puffy dress from the rack closest to him. "Ethan will like this."

"Oh, no," Miss Tight Ass says, rushing toward him. "That's for a child, for the flower girl. You need something becoming. Something that will cover your derriere."

She grabs the dress from Warrick and hangs it back on the metal bar.

The hanger makes a slight clink as it lands.

"I love that dress," I say.

"And she wouldn't need to push it aside when all the bikers make their move on her," Warrick says with a wink.

"Oh, my," Miss Tight Ass says. "Dear, you shouldn't let men treat you that way. And shame on this man for condoning such a thing."

"It's how it's done in our club," he says with a shrug. He doesn't budge when Miss Tight Ass tries to scoot around him, so she has to maneuver through a wall of satin fabric.

"Come with me, dear," she says, taking my hand in her cool, papery one. As she ushers me along, she seems to be protecting me.

I can barely keep from laughing. "I really like that little dress over there," I say, pouting. "It won't get in the way of moving. How am I supposed to move my legs in these long things?"

"This dress will be lovely," she says, taking what looks like miles of glossy fabric on a hanger from a rack. She holds the sleeveless dress up to my body and eyes it, whispering, "This one is perfect."

I look down and agree it's a lovely dress, even if it is the color of a bleached gator skull. "Can it be dyed a different color?" I ask.

"Different than white?" The woman looks shocked. "It's traditional to wear white."

"Do we look traditional?" Warrick calls from across the floor, where he's rolling a cigarette between his fingers. "Luna's been fucked every which way. She don't need any of that white bullshit."

The tinkling bells sound as another customer enters.

"Oh, no," Miss Tight Ass says, dropping the dress to scurry toward Warrick. "There's no smoking in here. You'll ruin these dresses. Ruin them!"

"What kind of a place is this?" he says, placing the smoke between his lips.

"Jacksonville's finest," she says, attempting to push him toward the door.

Of course, he doesn't budge. It's like a fly trying to shove an elephant. He strides toward me, pushing her out of the way.

She falls back into a rack of dresses.

The new customer stares at us. When her friend enters, they huddle together, pointing and whispering.

"This dress is so pretty," I moan, lifting the dress into the air.

"Is that the one you want, baby girl?" Warrick says as he stands before me.

"Yes," I cry. "I love it."

"But now it's all dirty," he says, brushing off some non-existent dirt. "Look at those fingerprints we've gotten on it. Let's get another one."

"I'll give you a discount," Miss Tight Ass says in her tight-lipped fashion, hurrying toward us.

The two women turn and exit the store.

"Can it be dyed purple?" I say.

"Anything... Anything you want as long as we get you out of here." She seizes the dress from my hands and fluffs it. "Let me ring you out over here."

She hurries toward the counter where her payment device is located.

Warrick removes his lighter and flicks it into flame.

"Outside with that," she cries.

He extinguishes the flame and saunters next to me. At the counter, he rests his forearms against the glass and says, "Will you have this delivered?"

The un-lit smoke bobs up and down between his teeth.

"Absolutely. Where would you like it sent?"

Warrick gives her the address, and she pales.

"What? You don't like people like us who live in those parts? You think we're uncivilized animals just because we turn into wolves?"

"We don't judge here," she says, her hands shaking as she taps the payment console. "All supernatural species are welcome."

"Sure seems like you judge," Warrick says.

I'm about to lose it and burst into laughter.

Paper spews from the device with the price on it.

"Did you discount that dress? It's dirty from your negligence," Warrick says.

Her lips press so tight I think they're going to shatter. She stabs the console repeatedly, and, again, paper spits out. She holds out the receipt for Warrick. "Here's your discount."

He peels several bills from the roll and hands them to her. "Keep the change. And we need the dress delivered tomorrow."

She sputters, then thinks better of it and closes her mouth. "That'll be fine.

"Thank you so much," I coo, batting my eyelashes.

Warrick tucks the cigarette into the pocket of his leather vest. "I wasn't going to light up," he says, glaring at the shopkeeper. "What kind of manners do you think I'm made of?"

Return to the Pack

I hook my arm in Warrick's elbow, and we exit the store.

Out on the sidewalk, we howl with laughter.

"Damn," Warrick says as we weave toward his motorcycle. "I haven't had that kind of fun in a while. Nice job playing along. I wasn't sure you'd catch on."

"I learned to play pretend with Ethan and Callan," I manage to say, unable to stop laughing.

"Don't tell me. I can only guess what those two came up with for a game." Still laughing, he climbs on his motorcycle and starts it up.

I clamber on behind him. "Where to next?"

"The lingerie store… We'll see what kind of fun we can have there," Warrick says with a grin.

God, how I love this guy. There's no one like Warrick. But then a lightning strike of fear quashes my good mood. What if I were to lose him… To lose any of the boys to those evil mutated wolves? That thought chills me to my core. We have got to find the maneaters and kill them before it's too late.

Chapter Sixteen

Luna

The entire ride home from Jacksonville, clinging to Warrick's torso, my brain has been scheming. Warrick and I had a blast in town, and I want to make sure he knows how much it means to me that he took me out today. We went shopping for a dress, shoes, makeup, lingerie—which I found out is just fancy underwear—and even a glittery crown called a tiara.

To show my gratitude, I intend to give Warrick so much pleasure his mind will explode.

When we finally get home, with stars twinkling in the sky, I enter the house while Warrick parks his bike in the garage.

"Hey," I say, finding Axel stretched out on the sofa, icing his leg, which healed but still hurts him if he works too hard building one of the houses for the pack wolves.

"Hey," he says with a smile, flipping the TV to mute and tossing the remote on the coffee table. "How was your day?"

"Oh, we had so much fun! We messed with a couple of store clerks, making up stories about how I'm going to get married in a biker's wedding. Fifty bikers are all going to have their way with me, and..." I start laughing again. "This one shopkeeper—I thought she would combust. All she wanted to do was to get rid of Warrick and me as fast as she could."

Axel pats the cushion next to him. "Sounds like fun."

"And then we went out for burgers, fries, and milkshakes. And then Warrick took me out on a long ride, soaring through the backroads. It was incredible." I settle next to Axel and take his hand. "Where are Callan and Ethan?"

"They crashed already," he says. "Today was brutal, but we got a lot done."

"You waited up for me?"

His expression falls and he tugs his hand away. "I thought I'd sleep on the mattress in the corner tonight. What about you? You'll probably sleep with Warrick after the day you two had."

"Probably," I admit. "I wish we had a bigger bed." I draw circles on Axel's chest. "We need a bigger bed and a bigger house—bigger everything."

"It's okay, Luna. We can't always be together. It's good to sleep apart sometimes." He picks up the remote and flips on the sound again.

I take the remote from his hand, mute the noise and toss it out of reach.

Warrick tromps into the front room. "What's this about sleeping apart? I thought I could keep you busy for a while, Luna."

He waggles his eyebrows as he steps toward the couch and scoops me into his arms.

Axel's jaw works side to side, and he reaches across the couch for the remote, flipping on the sound again.

Warrick slings me over his shoulder and heads for his bedroom.

"Hey," I say, pounding his back.

"What?" he says, slapping my rump. When we get to his bedroom, he slams the door and pitches me on the bed. Then, he falls next to me and starts peeling off my clothes.

"Warrick, wait," I say between squeals.

"Been waiting all day," he says, grabbing my waistband with his teeth and yanking my pants down my hips. "I'm about to suck my baby girl's pussy dry."

"I have an idea," I say, lifting my hips so he can tug them from my legs.

"Does it involve role play?" He shakes my pants in his mouth like they're prey, then tosses them from the bed.

"No, it involves Axel," I say.

His frenetic movements cease, and he stares at me, blinking. "It involves Axel how?"

"Here in bed with us, taking pleasure together."

Warrick wrinkles up his nose. "Nah, I'm fine with what we're doing."

My t-shirt's still on, but my ass is bare, so Warrick lowers his face between my legs and takes a long sniff. "Heaven," he says, spreading my thighs with his palms. And then he starts to lick me.

The sensation is exquisite. It's like our outing today served as foreplay. Before I get lost in pleasure, I wriggle my nails into his long hair and say, "Daddy, wait."

"What now?" he says, licking the taste of me from his lips.

"Axel... Can I ask him to play with us? He looked so sad. I need you to see how much I need both of you." I clasp my hand beneath my chin and bat my eyes at him. "Please, Daddy?"

He lets out a groan and collapses on the bed next to me. "Fine. Go ask him. But hurry." He rolls on his back, grabs his thick cock, and starts to pump it. "I'll be ready to finish in that tight little cunt when you get back."

I try to pry his hand away from his erection, but it's Warrick. And if Warrick doesn't feel like budging, he won't budge.

"Get a move on, sweetheart," he says with a grin. "And get that pussy wet on the way or it'll be a sore tomorrow for you."

"I'm moving, I'm moving." I scramble from the bed and hurry toward the front room.

Axel's lying on the mattress in the corner with his arm over his eyes.

"Axel," I whisper.

"What," he says in a grumpy voice.

I lower to my hands and knees next to him. "Want to play with us?"

He lowers his arm from his face and stares at me. "With you and Warrick? No, thanks."

"Come on…*please?*" I run my palm across his bare torso.

Axel chews his cheek. He shakes his head.

"Warrick's down with the idea."

Axel's eyes narrow as he regards me. "I highly doubt that."

"Warrick!" I yell.

"What?" he calls back.

"You're down to play with Axel, right?"

"Get on in here and find out," he yells. "But hurry the fuck up or I'll finish without you."

"Come on," I say, scrambling upright and grabbing Axel's hand. I drag him into the bedroom.

Once I'm next to the bed, I leap next to Warrick. He glances at Axel, then pulls me on top of his bulky body. "Are you playing, or what?" he says to Axel without looking at him.

Return to the Pack

Wordlessly, Axel climbs onto the bed next to Warrick.

An awkward silence fills the room. I slide from Warrick and nestle my body between the two men, tugging on Warrick's shoulder until he rolls to face me.

He slides a hand between my legs and thrusts his thick fingers into me, two at once. I whimper and tense up. "You can take it, baby girl," he says, grinning and plundering my pussy with his rough fingers.

Axel begins to stroke my back, my hips, my shoulders. His hands are sure, and his touch is loving, and I begin to relax.

Loving Warrick is like loving a bear—all bulk, and fur, and power.

Warrick's tongue plunders my mouth as he thrusts his cock against my belly. Then, he makes this low grunt in the back of his throat, like the bellow of a lion. "You're so fucking tight. Like my baby girl's still a virgin."

Axel slides the head of his cock between my ass cheeks. It glides smoothly, lubricated by his pre-cum, but each time it slides past my rear entrance, I tighten up. He wriggles closer to me and bites my neck, holding on with his teeth. His hand snakes around and finds one of my nipples, which he twirls and tweaks.

I gasp and rock my hips against him.

Warrick guides my leg over his hip, takes his cock, and slides it up and down my slick folds.

This allows Axel greater access, so he presses the head of his erection against the hole of my backdoor.

I suck in a breath and tense slightly, but he just waits there, like he's knocking before entering.

Warrick drives inside me with a grunt, distracting me.

"Warrick," Axel says.

"Yeah?"

"Hold up just one sec. I need Luna to relax so I can get in, too."

Warrick's cock pulses inside me, but he doesn't move his hips. Instead, he returns to my mouth and sucks, nibbles, and kisses me.

Axel whispers in my ear. "Relax. Open up, Luna, my mate."

I take a shuddering breath and allow myself to open.

Slowly, with exquisite care, Axel enters me.

It's an intense sensation, stretching me apart.

"Oh, fuck," Axel utters. "Can you feel this, Warrick?"

"What, your cock?" Warrick says against my mouth.

"Yeah," Axel says, but it sounds more like a groan. "Oh, fuck."

"I'm well aware." Warrick slowly thrusts inside me.

Axel barely moves, but I feel him deep inside.

Return to the Pack

I'm consumed with the sensation of these two powerful males loving on me, with me sandwiched between them. All talk ceases as we fall into the rhythm of pleasure. It's intense, and it's driving me mad. When Axel begins to move, claiming my asshole, Warrick groans and begins to pound into me relentlessly, his size making tears fall from my eyes as he grows rougher and rougher. Their cocks fill me again and again, stretching my ass and my pussy until I can barely stand it. I'm sobbing with pleasure and pain as Axel's hips meet my ass and his hand snakes around my body, tormenting my clit while Warrick jams his oversized cock so deep inside me it's torture.

Finally, I can hold it back no more. I scream as my body begins to spasm around both their cocks. Warrick bellows his release while Axel whispers dirty love talk into my ear. I come hard, too, crying and shaking as Warrick grinds so deep my whole body clenches.

"Sweet wolf spirit above," Axel moans as he lets go. I come again, blinded by the intense pleasure coursing through me. It rolls through me in waves.

When we all come down, Warrick rolls on his side, away from me, and pulls me close.

Axel whispers, "Be right back."

He slides away and rolls off the bed. I lay hugging Warrick as he starts to softly snore.

When Axel returns, the smell of soap wafts into the air. He rolls me onto my back and gently cleans me with a wet cloth, then rolls me over to clean my rear entrance, too. His soft touch and gentle care eases the sting of the soap and water on my tender flesh.

When he's done, he comes back to Warrick's bed instead of returning to the front room. I snuggle in, pulling him closer still. Then I drift away, cocooned in the arms of the two strongest males a girl could ever want.

Chapter Seventeen

Luna

It's one of those days in Florida when the weather is sublime, and the skies are clear. Not a single cloud mars the sky, and a light breeze gently plays with my hair. It's the perfect day for a wedding, now that I know what makes up a wedding.

I'm standing at the edge of the Creebay Preserve clearing with Elder Amexaryl, Adolpha, Kato's mate, Okami, and two little wolf children, waiting for my bridegrooms to arrive. Guests sit in chairs arranged beneath the trees, dressed in their finest clothes. There's an air of expectancy humming through the pack at this most unusual day when I am to take not one, but *four* mates. Sure, I've heard whispers of gossip and questions floating through the air, but no one's said anything unkind—not yet, anyway.

Adolpha has threaded purple orchids through my long hair, which has been re-dyed a bluer shade this time. I'm wearing the gown Warrick bought for me, which compliments the flowers and my hair both. It hugs my waistline, plunges to my navel, and cups my breasts, and I think my mates are going to howl when they see me.

I scan the road leading to the clearing, searching for signs of my lovers. Finally, a distant rumbling alerts me to their arrival, and a big, goofy grin spreads across my face. A few minutes later, three shiny motorcycles roar into view, leading the way for Axel's truck. The truck has been washed and polished, and flags of the Jacksonville wolf pack flap in each corner of the bed.

The motorcycles and truck pull up to the edge of the clearing. The boys rev their engines to the whoops and applause of the pack.

But the vehicles pale compared to their riders and driver who exit from their rides. All four men are dressed in their rented tuxedos with violet waist sashes—they called them cummerbunds—and bow ties.

Warrick and Callan's hair hangs glossy and abundant around their faces, while Ethan's short-cropped hair has the sign of the wolf shaved close to his skull. Axel's is combined back neat and shiny.

They can't see me behind Adolpha and Okami, but I can see them. The sight of them takes my breath away. They're all tall and muscular, exuding power and dominance that makes my wolf want to roll on her back and give them her belly.

Elder Amexaryl strides to the podium set before the guests and gestures for the men to follow. Her yellow robes billow about her body, tossed by the breeze. In her hand, she carries a staff with the teeth of fallen wolf warriors dangling from the end, clacking softly together.

She's radiating magical energy as she stands tall, waiting for the men to take their places.

They stand next to her with their hands clasped loosely before them, in the position of rank—Axel first, then Warrick, then Callan and Ethan.

"Ready?" Adolpha says, hooking her hand into my elbow.

I roll my lips between my teeth and nod my response, overcome with emotion.

"Girls," she says to the two children, dressed in their pretty white dresses with purple trim—I'm pretty sure one of them is the dress Warrick picked for me first at the shop.

The girls skip toward Elder Amexaryl, strewing wildflower petals on the ground.

Dressed in a loose-fitting dress to cover the baby bump in her belly, Okami follows them, herding them along.

Adolpha nods at me, her eyes glistening. "Let's go," she whispers.

We step into the clearing, and a hush falls over the crowd. All eyes are on me as I float toward my four mates.

Each one of them stares at me with emotion brimming in their eyes. Devotion clouds Axel's eyes.

Hunger radiates from Warrick. Ethan winks at me, wolf playfulness and mischief threading through the admiration in his gaze. Pure love shines through Callan's beaming smile.

When I reach the podium, Elder Amexaryl says, "Please surround your mate."

My men move around me until I'm cocooned in their masculine energy.

Elder Amexaryl reads a passage from a book on wolf lore. Then in a clear, rich voice, she performs the simple ritual. "Do each of you accept Luna as your sole mate, through love and laughter, through trial and tribulation, in wolfskin and human form, for all of your days on this earth?"

They all murmur their assent.

Axel adds, "In this life and beyond."

Elder Amexaryl nods. Then she looks at me and says, "Luna, do you accept Axel, Warrick, Callan, and Ethan as your sole mates..."

"I do," I say, unable to wait a moment longer to claim my mates.

Elder Amexaryl finishes the sentence and then lifts her staff and touches the wolf teeth to each of our heads. "And now, by the power vested in me by our holy wolf spirit, I pronounce you life mates."

Each of the men kisses me in turn until my cheeks are ablaze.

Then, Warrick grabs my waist and lifts me to his shoulder.

I let out a squeal.

Axel supports me on the other side.

Callan and Ethan take their places on either side.

"Congratulations," Borris shouts.

"Our pack is mighty!" someone else calls.

The pack folds around us until we're surrounded. Fiddles start playing, and two people begin to dance, then two more and two more until everyone is caught up in the music.

Someone reaches for me and sweeps me from Warrick and Axel's shoulders. I turn to see Hati, who grabs my hands and twirls me in a circle. Someone else moves in on Hati, and we skip through the crowd. Then Axel cuts in, places one hand around my waist and the other holding my hand, and we weave through the pack.

"I'm so in love with you," he says, smiling.

"Me, too," I say, grinning. "Or you, too? Which one is it?"

"I don't know," he says, laughing. "I just know I'm honored to be your husband."

Warrick slides in front of Axel. "My turn. Go play Alpha."

His tone of voice is warm, though, and Axel allows the intrusion.

Next, Callan and Ethan appear on either side of me and sweep me away from Warrick.

I don't think I've ever felt so happy.

A few of the women prepare the barbecue pit, setting it ablaze. Everywhere pack members are nibbling on snacks, drinking, laughing, and talking.

Thoughts of my mama and all she denied me whiz through my brain. For a moment, I'm flooded with compassion for her—in denying me access to the pack, she also rejected entry to the community. But I won't think a single bad thought today.

I fling my arms skyward and send all negative thoughts of her flying. Mama deserves to be free, wherever she is…and I deserve to be happy with a pack at last.

Chapter Eighteen

Warrick

We're hours into the festivities. I'm sitting on a tree stump next to my brothers. It's the best place for me to be right about now, since walking is difficult. I'm about to tip a bottle of whiskey to my lips and drain it dry. My limbs are loose, and my speech is slurred. Which accounts for not being on alert and sensing danger.

Suddenly, three huge shadows rocket into the clearing from the shadows of nightfall. I bolt to my feet and stumble backward, caught off-guard by their arrival. We've all been busy celebrating and intoxicating, letting down our guard and letting loose, working off the stress of the year.

Now, the enormous beasts loom over us, bounding into our festivities in the form of wolves that are three times the size they should be.

Chaos explodes all around me as women scream and run for their children, grabbing them and yanking them toward safety. One of the mutants launches for Kato, who stands next to me. Without time to shift, Kato falls to the ground, writhing and shouting.

I glance around wildly for my new mate, who's several yards away, sprinting away from the murderers. "Get Luna," I bellow to Ethan. "Get her the *fuck* out of here."

"On it," he shouts, already in motion.

I shift, shredding my rented tux to strips that fall away from my fur. I leap for the throat of the motherfucker attacking Kato.

That bastard wolf is twice my size and completely berserk.

I'm struggling for purchase on his neck when Axel leaps toward his other side.

Together, working as a team, we manage to take the maneater to the ground.

Axel shakes his head viciously, and the maneater's skin is torn from his neck.

Blood spurts from his veins, and his massive head and body fall with a thud to the ground.

Axel tugs Kato's limp body out of the way. Then he takes off to save someone else.

I sure hope Kato makes it, but none of us have time to check. I race after a maneater who's chasing Adolpha and manage to sink my teeth into one of his back legs before he can attack her.

Return to the Pack

He turns on me, and we roll over and over in a giant blur of snarling fangs and fur. If the first freak wolf was big, this one is enormous. He's too big for me, and he escapes, leaving me panting.

Thoughts whisper through my brain, and I realize Axel is telepathically issuing a command to my brothers and me, and the whole pack.

We've got to work as a team. They can't be brought down alone. Let's get into formation side by side and chase the bastards from our territory.

I send back my affirmation and hear the echoing assent from the pack through our bond.

I wheel around and see my brothers charging toward me. Pivoting, my gaze lands on three maneaters that are tearing two pack members, limb from limb. *This is war, baby!*

My brothers and I hurtle toward the motherfuckers.

Axel joins us, and we barrel toward the intruders.

Flank them, flank them! Axel commands.

We split into two groups on either side of the three wolves, slightly behind them.

Go for the legs. Hobble them.

Moving as one, Callan, Ethan, and I lunge simultaneously, seizing their back legs with bone-crunching fury.

The three wolves fall to the ground, their back legs in pieces.

I spit out fragments of bone and make eye contact with Axel.

The two ahead of us?

He nods and takes off, with the warriors in the pack in hot pursuit.

We work like this in tandem until all of the mutant wolves are either dead. Then, satisfied that we're safe, we shift back to humans.

Blood covers Axel's chest. It drips from Callan's neck and oozes down Ethan's arms. I glance at my torso, and I've got a few scrapes and gashes, but nothing major.

"Good work, everyone," Axel says, wiping the back of his hand across his blood-covered mouth. "I'm going to go check on the submissives back at the clearing. Callan, you and Ethan find Luna and make sure she's safe. Warrick, head over to the vampire's lair and warn them of impending danger. There could be more of these wolves in the area."

"You got it," I say.

Before I go, I glance around at the rest of the pack, some still in wolf form, some back to their human form. Everyone looks shaken and battered. A couple of the women weep over their too-still mates.

I shake my head. Those motherfucking mutants are going to pay.

Return to the Pack

"Let me take a look at your wounds, Axel," Callan says. "You look pretty beat up. Ethan, you take care of Luna. We'll join up with you once I've stitched Axel's wounds."

"I'm fine," Axel growls.

"You're too jacked on adrenaline to know if you're fine." He claps his hand on Axel's shoulder. "If it helps you feel like a man, I won't numb you up when I stick my needle into your skin."

"Asshole," Axel says, shrugging Callan off. "I've got to see to the pack."

"Macho alpha prick," Callan says, grinning. "You won't be around long enough if you don't let me stop the bleeding."

Leaving them to argue, I shift and lope toward vampires territory. Axel and I worked well together today. I think our baby-girl is a wise woman to have brought Axel into my bed. I feel as close to him today as I do with my brothers.

I increase my speed, loping across the dirt, skirting through trees and underbrush, using my senses and keen night vision to guide me on my way. I pick up the scent of wolves ahead and slow my speed. Then I lower myself to the ground and belly crawl toward the sound.

Ahead, the vampires are surrounded by the giant, foreign wolves.

Their fur is bloody. A few of them who got away from us bear the marks of our attack in the form of skin flapping from their necks and broken legs.

There's a slight problem here. There's only one of me.

The vampires are surrounded, held captive by the snarling muzzles of at least a dozen enormous mutant wolves with the strength of three of me, the rage of a man hopped up on steroids, and no apparent instinct for self-preservation.

Chapter Nineteen

Luna

Sometimes it stinks to be watched over like a wolf pup, and tonight is no exception. Adolpha and Okami keep me trapped in the back of Okami's van while the mutant wolves are destroying the pack—*my* pack. Since there are no windows in the back of her van, I can't even see what's going on. The only thing I can see is the road into town, which is where we're headed.

Ethan insisted we go to Adolpha's house, away from the attack.

I'm beyond anxious, wondering if the four men I just married are okay. I know we're supposed to share a telepathic connection, but I've only caught snippets. They checked in to see if I'm okay, and since then, I can only feel them, not hear clear thoughts. I can sense each of their life essences, but I'm new to this whole pack bond communication.

"You've got to stay calm and let the warriors deal with this," Adolpha says from the front passenger seat. "They train for this kind of thing."

"But my *mates*… What if one of them gets hurt?" I bite my fingernails, or what's left of them. They've been bitten to the quick already.

"Let's not go there," Omaki says. "Thoughts are things. Instead, let's give thanks for the strength of our warriors and let our affirmations increase their speed and stamina."

I don't know what she's talking about, so I focus on my beautiful purple wedding dress—it's got a tear in it. My hem caught something when I clambered into the van. I was being pushed, hustled, and hurried along by Adolpha, Okami, and Ethan before Ethan took off in a mad sprint for the fight.

Oh, well. The dress served its purpose.

The smells in this van are intense. It's a sour, rotting plant smell that makes me want to wretch. "What's the smell back here?"

"Oh, that," Okami says, chuckling. "You're smelling sauerkraut. We use the van for deliveries. Kato and I started a small home business a while back to help with expenses. It might smell funky, but it's yummy."

"If you say so," I say, wrinkling up my nose.

"Wolves making sauerkraut. Funny, isn't it?" Okami grins, making her petite features light up like the sun.

She's being nice, but I'm sure she's just babbling to keep me from fretting. It isn't working. Today was my wedding day, and those assholes just ruined it. I'm sure if they let me out of the van, I could kill one of the scary beasts for that reason alone.

The van comes to a stop. Adolpha climbs out of the passenger door. I wait while Okami exits the driver's seat and disappears for a few seconds until the back doors swing wide. "Out you go."

Her gaze glances nervously in the direction of the preserve, and it's evident she's as freaked as I am. She's just been doing her best to keep me calm.

I climb free from the van and follow Okami up the sidewalk.

Adolpha's already on the porch, digging in her purse for her keys. Glancing over her shoulder, she says, "Come on in. We'll lock the doors, shut the windows—whatever we have to do to stay hidden."

"Do you think the mutant wolves will follow us here?" I say with a shiver.

"Anything is possible," Adolpha says, her expression dark. "I don't know what they're after. Most wolves are honorable, and their warriors challenge ours if they want pack land or dominance... They'd never dream of hurting a submissive, male or female. Submissives are protected and treasured, as we bear the children to keep the pack lineage alive. But these wolves... I just don't know."

I don't like that statement at all.

"Because they already attacked me," I say quietly.

I hurry into the house after Adolpha and lock the door. I help her shutter all the windows. Then we wait…and wait…and wait some more. We don't talk much—the tension is high. But suddenly, my brain is tickled with a communication.

Get ready, baby-girl!

I start to grin—Warrick's on his way to get me. And when the familiar roar of a motorcycles approaches, I leap to my feet and run toward the window.

"Wait," Adolpha cries. "Don't open the shutters!"

Too late—I've already thrown them open.

I'm thrilled to see Warrick careening onto the front lawn. In one swift move, he parks the bike, leaps from the seat, and sprints toward the house. I unlock the deadbolt and swing it open before giving him a chance to hammer on it with his fist.

I gape at my Daddy—he's disheveled and bloody, but at least he's okay.

"Luna," he barks. "And you two. Let's get a move on. All wolves are needed. The vampires are surrounded, and we need to gather *everyone,* and I mean *everyone,* to fight. The war has begun."

He pauses mid-sentence and eyes Okami's swollen belly. "Except for you. No pregnant women."

"What's happening?" I ask.

"You'll ride with me, baby girl," Warrick says as he seizes my hand.

Together, we sprint across the lawn toward his motorcycle.

"Warrick, hand me your knife," I say once I'm standing near his bike. "I need to make some alterations."

He removes his long blade from the sheath on his belt and hands it over.

I slice the hem from my beautiful dress and rip the rest of it off so my legs are free.

Warrick grins as I hand the knife back. "Nice legs, baby girl. Can't wait to have them wrapped around my head tonight."

"Me, too," I say as I wait for him to climb on his motorcycle.

This time, however, he pats the seat between his legs. "I want you right here, baby girl, with my arms around you, keeping you safe."

His words land in my heart with a cascade of heartfelt emotion. I settle my rump in his crotch, leaning into his abdomen, and rest my palms on the curved handlebars.

He balances the bike on one leg and kicks the kickstand back with the other. Next, he holds the choke lever down and flips on the ignition. After that, he closes the choke and throttles the engine into a powerful growl. "Ready, baby girl?"

"Ready," I say, snuggled into him.

He stretches his long legs into the foot pedals, and we take off, speeding toward Creebay Preserve.

When we arrive at the preserve, Warrick turns off the engine and climbs off.

As I clamber from the motorcycle, Warrick says, "Let's go. Axel's at the front." He lifts his hand and points.

A sea of wolf-shifters stands before me, all waiting for instruction from their pack leader.

Axel's pacing back and forth, barking out orders while moving with a significant limp.

"Oh, no! What happened to Axel?"

"He got injured saving someone. But that's battle. You should have seen how well we all worked together," Warrick says, grinning, as he throws his arm around my shoulders and guides me through the crowd. "We're a force to be reckoned with."

"I'm sure you are," I say, pride filling my chest to be with four of the fiercest wolves in the land.

"My brothers are already on their way to the vampire's territory with the first flank of warriors." Warrick's long legs propel him forward with speed and strength as I trot to keep up with him. Finally, he scoops me into his arms and carries me the rest of the way.

We reach the front, and Warrick places me on the ground.

I hurry toward Axel.

Axel's face lights up, and he limps in my direction, pulling me into his arms for a quick embrace. "Damn, I'm glad you're safe."

"I wanted to fight beside you," I say, pouting at him.

He presses his palms on either side of my face and looks intently into my eyes. "You'll get your chance. You're going to stay close to me and the triplets, though, got it?"

I nod. "Understood. I'm ready."

"Good." He plants a quick kiss on my lips and turns to face the pack. Then, in a loud, clear voice, he calls, "Let's shift and move out."

It's like witnessing a gigantic explosion to see so many werewolves shift at once. Within seconds we're all fang and fur, loping toward our destination, the territory occupied by the vampires.

I feel powerful as I lope between two of my men, on my way to the other two.

The scents of the swamp are always one hundred times more potent when I shift into a wolf. I can smell the swamp mice, owls, snakes, and gators. The foliage comes alive with different aromas. Each plant and animal carries a distinct odor, and they all mesh together to form one giant scent cocktail.

All too soon, though, the scent of blood invades my nostrils. When we arrive, we come upon a scene of carnage. Giant wolves are tearing apart the vampires.

Vampire body parts lay strewn across the bog. They're supposed to be immortal, but no one can put together this unrecognizable mashup of flesh and bone.

A message comes through my thoughts, a quick order.

Surround them. Work in teams. Don't let a single maneater get past.

Working as one, the pack spreads out and surrounds the mutant wolves and vampires. I stick close to Axel and Warrick—while I might talk a good talk, I'm scared of the terrifying, oversized wolves attacking everyone.

They appear to be fearless, hell-bent on killing everything in their sight, and not at all deterred by thoughts of their own mortality.

I don't know how we're going to do it. We might be mighty in number, but the hybrid wolves are crazed. And as far as I can tell, none of the Jacksonville wolf pack ever prepared to fight against maneating, drugged-up giants.

Chapter Twenty

Luna

Go for the legs, Axel urges in my head as he, Warrick, and I herd one of the mega wolves toward the swamp which lines the vampire's territory.

I lunge, feeling the satisfaction as my teeth connect with bone and muscles. The tang of bitter blood fills my mouth, and I shake my head with fury.

The giant wolf, whose leg is in my grip, snarls, and scream, turning on me.

Axel and Warrick go for either side of his throat.

In seconds, the maneater lays still on the ground.

We take off for the next mutant—the one with his teeth around Drake's leg.

Drake's face is clenched in a rictus of pain. His fangs extend, and he tries to seize the mutant's muzzle to pry his leg free. The wolf clings to Drake's leg like he's fused his teeth with the vampire's bones.

We dive in, tearing at the mutant wolf's hind end. Axel and Warrick are like two killing machines, and I'm glad they're on my side, even if our opponents are bigger and stronger.

The massive wolf rips its leg from my teeth. Another lupine freak slams into me from the side, knocking the wind out of my lungs. As I struggle to catch my breath, he grabs my neck and bounds away.

I start to call for the others, but I don't want to distract them and get them killed. The wolf whose teeth are clamped firmly on my neck is the most enormous one I've ever seen in my life—no way will I be able to overpower him, but maybe I can outwit him or get free and outrun him.

My legs flail and kick as I'm being dragged across the sand by my neck. We're out of sight of the others before the hybrid wolf giant drops me. He plants his feet firmly on the ground, lowers his head, and snarls at me. The sound is vicious and deadly. I'm afraid to even breathe, let alone break eye contact with him. If I do, I'll be dead in two seconds flat.

And then a strange thing happens.

A voice, not the triplets and not Axel's, slithers into my brain.

Tastes. So. Good.

I blink, staring at the mutated wolf who has me trapped. *Are you communicating with me?*

I swear that fucker grins at me, but another low snarl leaves his throat.

Return to the Pack

You... Taste so good. I haven't tasted your bloodline for almost twenty years. But a wolf never forgets his first taste of human flesh. I've had your blood before. It's like nectar-infused water.

How is it I can hear you? I demand of the giant, trying to stall him. I'm afraid to call for the others now, since he'll hear it and surely kill me if I do.

I used to be in the Jacksonville pack. They found out I killed one of ours and ate him to hide the evidence. They knew I'd grow stronger, that I could challenge the Alpha with my new strength and take over. They banished me on the spot, but I ran before they could dissolve the bond.

His word hit me like bullets. Axel said the maneaters had killed my father, that the pack had trouble with them years ago. He didn't say they were from our pack!

When I was banished, I was alone. At first, I didn't know I'd grow stronger. They don't want you to know, so they don't tell you that. But I grew bigger and more powerful, and I figured out why. So, I consumed even more humans, and look at me now! I found others like me, outcasts and lone wolves, and I showed them how to be stronger than they could be even with a pack. The pack lies to you, little she-wolf. You don't need them to be strong. You only need the diet they forbid. If they allowed it, you'd be strong like me.

He stops the telepathy and slowly licks my blood, shuddering as he does so.

Suddenly, I'm consumed with rage. Rage that my father's dead because of maneaters, that my mother's stories about trusting the pack weren't all lies—my father was killed by the pack, just like she said. And most of all, I'm furious at Axel for lying to me. I feel utterly betrayed.

Awareness dawns on me, and every hair on my body stiffens. This exact wolf said he'd tasted my bloodline, that he'd never forgotten the taste since his first kill. The motherfucker standing before me is the same wolf who killed my father, effectively destroying my mother's and my lives. Fury burns through me like a hurricane of fire.

Without thinking, I launch into an attack, going for his neck, his face, whatever I can get my teeth on.

He meets my attack, and we roll over and over, all fang and fury until I'm laying in a heap in the sand, breathing hard, barely able to catch my breath. I'm no match for an overgrown freak who grew giant from eating his own kind.

He places a paw the size of one of a dinner plate on my ribcage and growls. *You can't win, sweetheart.*

I'm not your sweetheart!

I wriggle and writhe beneath his paw to no avail. It's like an anvil on my chest.

You soon will be…I'm going to eat your flesh and then feast on your bones. You'll make one hell of a tasty meal, and I'll be that much stronger. And I'll enjoy every delicious bite. Your bloodline tastes like honey. He makes a rumbling sound in his throat like a wolf-chuckle.

Return to the Pack

Still keeping me pinned to the ground, he lowers his head and licks the sanguine liquid flowing from my neck. I kick and flail until he places his other paw on my belly. He's so heavy and so strong I can barely breathe from the weight of him.

I want to cry, I want to howl, I want to *kill* him. I was married to four of our packs' greatest warriors today, but it feels like a dream. I didn't even have one day to be their wife, and now I'm going to die, leaving them without a mate.

The maneater laps my blood, growling with pleasure. I'm helpless to stop him. Soon, this asshole will tear me apart limb from limb, growing even stronger. Maybe he will challenge Axel now. Maybe he'll win, and the pack will belong to a savage cannibal. And Axel will be dead.

So it doesn't matter if the giant kills me. It's better for him to kill me than to kill my mate and eat the pack's weakest members one by one until only mutant wolves remain. So I close my eyes and summon all the strength I possess, and I unleash it.

Axel! I scream in my mind. *Help me!*

Chapter Twenty-One

Axel

All around us lies the evidence of war, in the form of dead pack members and vamps, dying wolves and giant maneaters desperately trying to kill us all. The vampires fight wickedly, trying to protect their own. My pack fights like the warriors they are—relentlessly, without mercy, using cunning and strategy as their weapons.

The land is drenched in blood.

Warrick, Callan, Ethan, and I have just vanquished another one of these giants jobs when a scream ricochets through my mind.

Help me!

The cry lances my heart like a sword, and I scan my surroundings wildly. Luna's gone. How could this have happened? She was just here, fighting side by side with us.

I sprint toward the call without another thought in my mind. Luna, my Luna, the heartbeat to my existence, is in danger. If I don't get to her in time...

Return to the Pack

I rocket away from the fight in the direction of her silent pleas. As my legs carry me, my head whips from side to side, searching for her scent.

When I find her, she's deep in the underbrush, and the largest maneater I've ever seen is tearing at her neck.

My vision turns red, hot with rage, and there's only one thought in my mind. I'm going to destroy this fucking wolf if it's the last thing I ever do. I'm like a missile as I launch at the beast.

He yips as if surprised by the attack, and then turns on me, going for my throat.

You're dead, Alpha.

Stunned by the communication, I falter, and his teeth connect with my flesh, grasping my foreleg.

You're nothing but a puppy.

This bastard is communicating with *me*. How is this possible?

Adrenaline pumps through my body, and I wrench my leg out of his grip and bite down on his throat.

Suddenly, Luna's at his hindquarters. Her sharp fangs sink into his muscles, and she rips and shreds with vicious shakes of her head. Finally, she pulls off a chunk of his leg, flings her head, and sends it flying. Then, she goes for the tender juncture between his hind leg and his belly. It's right at his groin, and it's one of the most sensitive parts of anybody, animal or human.

Blood spurts from his abdomen.

No, he screams. *The bitch is mine.*

Wanna bet? I rip out a chunk of his throat, and more blood spurts from his neck. I sink my teeth in and tear through his jugular, spraying blood as I sever it completely.

Soon, the bastard lays quivering in the sand. With a last puff of air, he stills.

I turn toward Luna, expecting to soothe her, but she launches at me.

Her communication screams through my mind.

You knew! You fucking knew!

Knew what? Luna, what are you talking about? I'm scrambling to keep away from her teeth. Has she lost her mind?

I don't want to do it, but I overpower her, pinning her to the ground under me. She's already wounded, so I'm careful not to use too much force. *Shift,* I command.

No.

Shift, goddamn it.

No!

Luna, obey my command.

I place my teeth around her throat in a threatening pose, but I don't break the skin. Still, the salty, sweet taste of her fills my mouth from where the other wolf bit her. For the first time, I use my dominance on her, forcing her submission.

She shifts and glares at me in all her glorious nakedness. "You knew, Axel. How could you keep this from me?"

I keep myself on top of her. *"Keep what?"* I ask through our bond.

"This wolf!" She stabs her finger in the air in the direction of the dead mutant.

"What about him?"

"Oh, sure, act like you don't know," she says.

I eye the blood seeping down her neck. I want to lick it and comfort her, closing the wound.

"Don't even think about comforting me," she snarls. "You're nothing but a liar and a betrayer."

Anger launches into my throat at her challenging my honor. *"You're going to have to come up with some facts to support your claim, Luna."*

"Are you going to stand there and tell me you don't know who this is?" she yells.

"I don't know who that is."

She whacks my chest with her palms, punctuating each word she speaks. "He. Killed. My *father*. And he was a pack member—*this* pack."

"What?" My gaze ping-pongs between the dead wolf and Luna.

"You had to know," she says, adding more whacks to my chest. "You weren't the Alpha eighteen years ago, but you were a member of the pack. You must have been a teenager then."

"I didn't know it was him," I growl. *"I only knew there was a fight between two wolves. Your father died and the other was banished, and your mother fled the pack and became a lone wolf."*

Her eyes narrow into slits. "But you knew it was someone from your pack!"

Now she starts pounding on me with her fists. I seize her wrists to stop the assault.

She writhes and squirms, kicking at me in an attempt to get free. She arcs back her head and tries to clock me in the forehead, but my paws stop her.

"I didn't know they were still alive or that they'd ever return for you. Hell, we didn't know you existed. Your mother severed the pack bonds and ran away without telling anyone she was pregnant."

Fat tears slide down her cheeks, breaking my fucking heart.

"Why didn't you tell me?"

"He was banished," I say. *"It's not something a pack likes to think about, that we had a cannibal among us. The pack was so ashamed that our alpha at the time ordered us to never speak of it, think of it... By his command, the events were cast from our memories and nearly ceased to exist."*

I lick her face, trying to comfort her.

"But he didn't cease to exist," she says with a sniffle. "He came back."

She shakes her head, knocking lose more tears. "You *knew*, Axel. You knew."

"I didn't know him at the time. He was an older member of the pack, and I was a kid, horrified when I learned of it. I didn't want you to fear joining the pack for no reason. He's not in it and hasn't been since before you were born. But you were so fearful..."

"You didn't think it was relevant?" she says in a voice laced with pain.

The shards of her words lance my chest. "I was only trying to protect you. The pack can do that. If they hadn't been here today, you'd be dead."

"I was never given a chance to choose for myself," she whispers, her head still shaking back and forth.

"I didn't know he'd come back," I assure her. *"He was banished, and we never heard from him again. We were ordered to never speak of him or his despicable acts. I've only wanted to protect you and keep you safe, have you as my wife and part of my pack."*

"By not telling me the truth," she says in a dead-sounding voice. Her hands grow limp in my grip, and she meets my gaze with her teary eyes. "I knew nothing of this, of what happened to my father. Mama never told me a thing. All I knew growing up was that belonging to a pack meant belonging to something evil. I'm starting to think she was right. If being part of a pack means being fed lies to keep you safe..."

Panic hammers against my heart. *"It doesn't,"* I assure her. *"We just got married—all of us. We're happy now.*

You can't leave, Luna. Not now. Not when you could have a baby in your belly like your mama. Please don't make the mistake she did. I promise I'll never withhold the truth from you again. You have my word."

She gives one last shake of her head, shoves me off, jumps to her feet, and races away.

Pain floods me inside, covering my thoughts with a landslide of grief.

As Luna disappears into the brush several yards ahead, I bolt after her. I find her wading into the swamp, her arms hanging limply from her side. I rush forward, pouncing on her, and we flounder into the murky water.

"I *trusted* you, Axel," she cries. "And you lied to me! Again!"

We fall back into the shallow water, and she wraps her arms and legs around me to keep herself from the water.

"I know, sweetheart. I know. And I let you down."

"I gave you my everything. I committed to sharing my life with you," she says, kicking at my sides with her heels. "I let you in."

I deserve this. I deserve everything she's giving to me. *"I know. I fucked up. You were so broken when I found you—so mistrusting. All I wanted to do was protect you and keep you safe. You can let me in. I promise. Let me in again."*

I stagger up onto the bank and lick her face, and she's still crying but she arches up against me.

Return to the Pack

"Shift," she says, panting and squirming against me. I realize she wants to fuck, and I'm only halfway shifted when she grabs my cock and thrusts up against it. I sink into her, needing the connection more than I've ever needed anything in my life. My hind paws dig into the mud as I thrust deep inside her slick little pussy. She gasps, her head falling back, her eyes closing in bliss. This is how we bond, how we come back to each other, every time. Our relationship might be volatile, but this is always right between us.

The muddy swamp bottom gives way beneath my claws, and we both slide deeper, but we don't separate. I lick her cheeks, swiping her tears away as I pump my cock deep inside her, my hulking form driving her pale little body down into her soft mud with each rough thrust.

"I loved you, Axel." Her face is swollen and flushed as she stares at me with eyes of betrayal and a broken heart. But she opens her thighs wide, lifting her hips to let me go deeper.

"Don't you love me anymore?" I say, my heart threatening to beat from my chest, my cock straining inside the tight grip of her shaved little pussy.

A beat lasting a lifetime stretches between us. I grind deep inside her, holding back as I feel my knot stretching her until she can't bear it. Her sheath begin to clench rhythmically around my cock, and her arms flail, churning in the shallow water as I thrust against her cervix a few times.

"I don't want to love you," she whimpers. "But God help me, I still do. I love you, Alpha."

Hearing those words makes me lose all control. My cum explodes into her, and I throw back my head and roar as my cock throbs so hard I see stars. Her cunt grips me in a second wave of orgasm, sucking and milking every drop from my engorged member. We're shaking with the power of it before her grip on my cock loosens and my knot contracts enough for me to slip from her. I finish shifting into my human form and pull her onto the bank again.

There, I press my hands on either side of her face. "Let me make it better. Let me try again. I promise to never lie to you again. To never withhold the truth from you, even if I'm afraid to share." I kiss her eyelids and her temples. I kiss her cheekbones and her chin. Finally, I make my way to her mouth, and she yields to me, kissing me with all the tenderness of a submissive mate.

The trees shudder with movement like bull elks are heading our way.

"Yo, Axel," Warrick bellows.

Luna and I slowly pull away from one another.

A terrible thought ricochets through me. I left the fight—I left everyone to save my heart.

The outlaw triplets thunder through the trees, and I scoop up Luna and stand.

"We kicked their asses," Warrick says, his chest puffing with pride. They're all covered in tattoos and blood—a dozen injuries marr their thickly muscled bodies, and blood soaks their beards and runs down their chins and chests from where they tore into the wolves. But they look like they'll all make a full recover. I'm surprised by the strength of my relief and happiness at that knowledge.

"It was epic," Ethan says.

"Tell me," I order. I kiss the top of Luna's head as I step through the sticky mud, heading for solid earth where they stand.

"The war..." Warrick says, beaming with pride at his prowess in battle. "It's over."

Chapter Twenty-Two

Luna

"We ripped those motherfuckers' heads off and ate their hearts out," Warrick bellows, shaking his shaggy head as we forge through the woods, heading back to the battleground.

He's dripping with blood, and there are scrapes and bruises everywhere.

"We were all engaged in battle." Warrick sweeps his hand through the air. "Callan was dragging a dying mutant freak by his tail. Ethan and I were double-teaming another, about to tear his throat apart from both sides. And then others started running to help us. We looked up, and we had the last two living mutants who hadn't turn tail and run."

He holds aside a branch for me to duck under.

"You did good," Axel says, unwilling to release my hand. That's okay with me because I don't want to let go of him, either. We just went through something epic, and the bonds between us are stronger than ever. I can feel him pulsing through my bloodstream like a rushing river.

"Yeah, I didn't know where the fuck you went," Ethan says to Axel, with one raised eyebrow. "But then I heard Luna's call, and I knew."

He gives me the warmest look that turns my bones into jelly.

"So, what happened?" Callan says to me.

I gave him a brief synopsis of what just went down, omitting all the pain and rage I experienced when I thought Axel had betrayed me.

"Holy fuck," Callan exclaimed. "So that was the asshole who started this whole thing?"

"Seems so," I say.

"By killing your father?" Ethan says, stepping over a log.

I nod. "Apparently. When that wolf ate him, he became strong. Then he convinced others to join him and eat more humans and wolves."

"And you knew about this, dude?" Warrick says to Axel.

"I knew one of ours killed her father," Axel says. "I fucked up. I didn't know it would make him come back for her, or I'd have told everyone."

"I'd say that's an important fact to share," Callan says, frowning.

"It wasn't relevant, but I've paid for keeping it from Luna," Axel says, releasing my hand with a scowl. "And I'm guessing I'll keep paying."

"Oh, no, you don't," I say, snatching his hand before it reaches his side. "We worked it out. Axel made a mistake. We *all* make mistakes."

"Except for me," Ethan says, grinning.

"Asshole," Axel says, slugging him in the arm.

"Hey," Ethan protests, still grinning. "That's one of my best attributes."

I smile at him. "If all the maneaters are gone, I want to put all this behind me and move forward. Are we in agreement?" I say, meeting each of their gazes as they turn to glance at me.

"Yes, little mama," Ethan says, giving me a mock salute. He throws his arm around my shoulder on the side opposite Axel. "So, you killed the last giant freak, huh?"

"We sure did," Axel says. "Luna got the first kill strike. She got him right here." He points to the juncture between leg and belly where I bit the wolf.

"Oh, shit," Callan says, cringing. "That had to hurt. You probably tore his femoral artery."

"It started spurting blood like a fountain," I say, grinning with pride.

"I'll bet it did," Callan says, smiling back at me with just as much pride as I feel.

Ethan drops his arm so I can scoot past a tree. I keep a steady grip on Axel, though. I don't want to let go of him.

Return to the Pack

We all come to a stop when we step from the underbrush. Dead, eviscerated bodies—vampire, maneaters, and members of the wolf pack alike—lay everywhere. The injured lay moaning or silently suffering, writhing in the sand. The wolves who emerged relatively unscathed have all shifted back to their human skin. Some slump on the ground, their arms over their knees or lean against trees, utterly fatigued, while others are bandaging the wounded.

The vampires cluster in a circle, their heads bowed. Drake looks up from the circle and calls out to us. "We need to talk."

Axel nods.

Warrick looks down at me. "You, baby-girl, need to find somewhere safe while we confer with the vamps."

"I want to meet with them, too," I say, my spine stiffening. I turn to Axel. "Can I stay?"

Warrick places his large hands on my shoulders. "No. Absolutely not. Just because we united to fight a common enemy, they're still *vampires*—our sworn enemies. It could be a trap."

"Please, Daddy?" I ask, batting my eyelashes at him.

"I think she should be allowed to attend," Axel says, and my heart swells with gratitude. "She's the Alpha's wife, and the Second's wife. She should know pack business, and it's good to have a few submissives temper our natures in negotiations like this."

"Thank you," I say to him. "He's right. I need to find my place in the pack, not just our family. You may be the Second, Warrick, but it's my pack, too."

"Fine," Warrick grits out, placating me with his palms facing forward. "Far be it from me to get in the way of my baby girl's powers of persuasion."

"Yeah, Luna, you're a powerhouse," Callan says. "No one can deny you anything."

Their support fills me with pride, and I beam at all my rough and bloody men. "Then let's go talk to some vampires."

We tromp toward them as a mighty team, connected with one gigantic beating heart.

Once we're standing in front of them, Axel pulls himself to his full, imposing Alpha height. "What do you need to say?"

He says the words calmly, but I can tell he's poised and ready for battle, if it comes to that, even though we're all exhausted.

Drake steps away from the circle with Evan by his side. Drake's pants leg is stained crimson, but he holds himself tall, too.

"We owe you our lives, Alpha," Drake says, meeting Axel's gaze with his dark, dead eyes.

"Go on," Warrick says, crossing his arms over his chest.

"We were certain you were responsible for the attacks on our human feeding stations and us. Even when you came to warn us of the maneaters, we were suspicious of your intent. Please accept my apology on behalf of my clan. I, for one, wouldn't be standing here today were it not for your warriors." Drake nods his head in a show of respect and Evan does the same.

Axel's face appears impassive, but I know his wheels are turning a mile a minute. "Thank you. We accept your apology on one condition."

"Of course," Drake says, one eyebrow raised imperiously. "You wouldn't be the Alpha if you weren't always negotiating for your pack."

"I want our land back," Axel says evenly. "Our pack land belongs to all our people, not just me. It is sacred to our people, and I gave it under duress when my mate was in danger. As a show of good faith between our people and yours, I would ask for it to be returned."

Drake looks down his nose at Axel, but I think he looks impressed. "It speaks to your devotion," he says coolly, his gaze sliding toward me. "A sacrifice for one's mate is a noble one."

My chest puffs at his words, but I school my emotion into neutrality and wait for the vampire's answer just as my mates do, with dignity.

After a long beat, Drake locks eyes with Axel. "Your land is yours, as payment rendered for your warning, and for defeating the hybrid wolves beside us."

"That's most generous," Axel says. "May this usher in a new era of peace between our peoples."

"Yes," Drake says. "In addition, we do not hunt game as you do. If you're in need of hunting grounds in the wake of the damage from the hurricane, we'll allow you access to our land for those purposes." He folds his arms over his chest and rises to his full height, displaying his arrogance like a peacock's tail.

Axel dips his head at the vampire leader. "In return, we'd like to offer you access to the same. You may feed from humans in our territory, as long as they are consenting."

"Of course," Drake says with a smirk. "Thank you, Alpha."

They nod their heads to each other, and then the vampires turn and shoot off through the trees in a blur, disappearing from view in seconds flat.

My men and I all start talking at once.

"Axel, you did it!" I say, jumping up and down.

He catches me in his arms and smooches me hard on the mouth.

"Good job, man," Warrick says, clapping him on the back.

Return to the Pack

Axel sets me down and smiles at me with a look of purest love. "You're going to get your dream house, Luna love."

"That I get to share with all of you," I reply, beaming at my men.

"Aw, shucks," Callan says. "Don't make me cry, pet."

With joy in our hearts for each other, we turn to the somber task that precedes the building of our home—burying the dead and restoring the injured in the pack. If anyone's capable of undertaking the job, it's the five of us, the toughest wolves in all of Jacksonville.

Chapter Twenty-Three

Luna

A few days later, we prepare to head back to our home at the triplets' cabin. We've been crashing at Adolpha's in her living room, tending to the dead and the grieving, but now, it's time to leave.

"It's been an honor housing our Alpha," Adolpha says with a smile as she bids us farewell. "You all seem to complement each other so well. I'm glad you forged new territory and got married. The pack will be stronger for it."

"Thank you," Axel says. "Coming from you, that means a lot."

Out in the sunshine, we stand before our respective vehicles. I'll ride with Axel in his truck, and the triplets will take their bikes.

"We need to stop at the mall before we head home," Callan says, with a sly wink at Ethan.

Warrick scoffs.

"Why's that?" I say, pausing before climbing into the passenger side.

"It's a surprise," Callan says, waggling his eyebrows.

"Yeah, take your time getting home," Ethan adds. "We have a few things to do before you arrive."

Intrigued, I turn to Axel and lace my fingers with his. "We can think of something to do, can't we?"

We've all been touchy and lovey since the battle. I think we're all just relieved and grateful that we're all safe and well. Our wolves healed our injuries, and now we're all as good as new, and married to boot.

"I hope you won't be too disappointed if it's pack business," he says. "I have to meet with Kato before we head out of here, see how he's healing."

"Of course," I say. "There will be plenty of time to play later."

He smiles down at me with gratitude and kisses me before lifting me into the passenger seat of the truck.

"Have fun getting your secret supplies," I say with a wave at the triplets.

Warrick gives me a salute, and the three of them roar down the street on their motorcycles.

The business Axel has to address takes about an hour. Axel insists I come in, since I'm an important member of the pack, but in truth, all the strategic planning bores me. At last, Axel sees my fidgeting and sends me out back with Okami to pick flowers from her garden. It's a huge patch with all different colors and varieties.

Okami insists I pick a huge bouquet to grace our dining room table at home. It makes me remember my sweet little house and how much pride I took in decorating it. The triplets' house is great, but it could use some prettying up.

"Those are beautiful," Axel says when we come in from the garden and find the business meeting over. "But not as pretty as you are."

I beam up at him, and he takes my hand and leads me out to the truck. We trundle down the road, chatting about everything. Before I know it, we're home.

As soon as I step from the truck, I smell delicious scents coming from the kitchen. I flash Axel a narrow-eyed look as I hug the flowers to my chest. "This is a setup, isn't it?"

"I don't know what you mean," he says, the picture of innocence.

I race toward the house and throw open the screen door to the kitchen.

"Surprise!" Ethan hollers, hopping off the step-stool where he was hanging pink and gold crepe paper.

A large banner hangs across the entrance to the front room. It reads, "To Us!"

Callan stands at the stove, stirring something flavorful in a large pot. A chocolate cake sits cooling on the counter.

"What's all this?" I ask.

"It's our honeymoon," Warrick says, striding into the kitchen. He scoops me and the flowers into his arms and kisses me soundly. Then, he places me back down on the floor.

"What's a honeymoon?" I ask, all flushed and excited from the kiss.

Candles sit in the middle of the kitchen table, along with a vase full of water for the flowers. Besides the banner and crepe paper, balloons bounce from the ceiling, reading, "It's a celebration!" and "Congratulations!"

"It's where you hide away and have sex, eat, have more sex, eat some more, and have sex again," Callan says over his shoulder.

"How fun!" I cry. "Those are my favorite things. I love honeymoons!"

I whirl in a circle and step toward the table where I deposit the bouquet. Ethan grabs my hand and pulls me into his arms. "A celebration calls for music. What do you say? Want to help me pick something?"

In the front room, we flip through ancient vinyl records and old CDs, searching for the perfect music mix. When we find it, we start dancing, bouncing around the room, leaping onto the couch, and jumping for joy.

Axel steps into the room and stands in the door watching until I grab his hand and drag him into the room, forcing him to dance with me. Callan hears the commotion and joins, and Warrick stands in the door, watching me with a lust-filled gaze as I wiggle my hips and shimmy to the muic.

When dinner is ready, we make our way into the kitchen.

Callan sets a platter of fish stew in the middle of the table with sourdough bread.

As I nibble a piece of bread, I eye each man, anticipation churning in my belly.

"What is it, Luna?" Axel asks, laying a gentle hand on mine. "You usually wolf down your food. Are you feeling alright?"

"I think so," I say shyly. "But I have an announcement."

They all start banging their spoons against their glasses. "Luna has an announcement," Ethan bellows. "Hurrah!"

When they quiet, I set down my utensils and flatten my palms on the table. "I haven't been feeling so good for a few days," I say. "And then I missed my moon."

"Are you saying what I think you are?" Axel asks intently, looking like he might pounce over the table at me.

I nod. "I think… I'm pregnant."

Ethan whoops. "That's fantastic!"

Callan wipes his eye and pretends the pepper in our food is making him tear up.

"We're going to be dads," Axel says, staring at me. Suddenly he jumps up, wraps his arms around me, and twirls me around and around. "I'm so happy, sweet Luna."

When he sets me down, I turn to Warrick, my stoic mate. "What about you, Daddy?" I ask, sliding onto his knee and wrapping my arms around his neck. "Are you happy your baby girl is having a baby?"

"So fucking happy." He puts his hands around my rump and guides me up onto his lap, straddling him. His cock is rock-hard and enormous against my pussy.

"Is this the part where we get to have sex before we eat some more?"

"Abso-fucking-lutely," he says.

With my legs wrapped around his hips, he carries me into the bedroom and lays me on his king-sized bed.

"What about the others?" I ask.

"Get your asses in here, and let's start honeymoon," Warrick bellows. "Or I'll fuck our baby girl full of pups all over again."

As the others file in, strip me bare, and worship every inch of my young body, I know I've got to be the luckiest wolf in the world. Four amazing older men to teach me the way and love me the way I love them, as only we can, with full love and acceptance of who we are. Life thrumming through my veins, safe now that all the threats to us have been eliminated. A baby in my belly who will grow up loved and with plenty of room to run. And the promise of a lifetime of happiness as we bring the next generation of wolves into the world.

Epilogue

Luna

Five years have passed since that terrible time when giant, maneating wolves almost destroyed the pack, the vampires, my men, and me. But in those five years, so much has happened. First, we reclaimed the packland from the vampires. Axel and our family took the clearing he'd envisioned as the perfect place for our family.

The lair the vampires had designed and started to build was too froufrou for our tastes. They wanted a winding staircase and crystal chandelier kind of dwelling. We used the framework and existing structure the vampires had already started to build a roomy, spacious home to *our* liking—simple, spacious, and functional. That's what we got, thanks to my men building it themselves. It's beautiful inside and out, with plenty of light and flowers always on the table.

Today I stand in the doorway, leaning against the frame, tea in hand as I watch Ethan pushing our son on the rope swing hanging from the Tupelo tree.

"Harder, Daddy," our fearless firstborn yells, laughing and kicking his legs.

"That's what your mother says," Ethan jokes, but the adult innuendo goes right over our child's head, thank goodness.

"Push me higher!" Aidan bellows.

Callan and Axel are trying to teach our three-year-old to play catch, while Warrick is pretending to ignore the four-year-old who is "helping" him work on his bike in the driveway.

A lovely little stream gurgles as it runs alongside the yard. The kids love to "go fishing" in the stream with their daddies. "Go fish" consists of everyone shifting and wading in the creek to try to snap up the crawdads as they scurry under rocks—everyone but baby Gavin, that is. Gavin's our toddler, and he usually occupies a place on my hip or at my side. With four men competing to see who can fill me with most seed every time I come into heat, I've gotten pregnant every time. I've been with child most of the past five years, but I don't mind. My men wait on me hand and foot for nine months and help raise our children the way they wish their parents had raised them.

"Where's Gavin?" I yell, searching for the two-year-old.

"He was right...." Axel's head swings back and forth. "Damn it. Gavin! Where'd you go, buddy?" he calls, exiting the game.

A loud splash sounds, and a child's wails follow.

Axel charges toward the stream. He wades in the ankle-deep water at the edge and fishes the toddler out by his shirt. "What did mommy tell you about playing near the stream?" he asks, bouncing Gavin on his hip to calm his fears. Gavin keeps crying, so Axel swings him up in the air until his wails turn into peals of laughter.

Ethan calls, "Let's head in and see what your mother's up to. Sound good, boys?"

Gavin cries, "Mommy! I want mommy!"

When Axel sets him down, Aidan takes Gavin's chubby hand and leads him toward the house.

The four men lumber along behind.

"I could use a cold beer. Who's with me?" Warrick states, wiping the sweat from his brow. We all agree in unison.

Our four-year-old races toward me, fast as his little legs will carry him. "Mommy!" he says, after colliding with my thighs.

I reach down to ruffle his golden curls. I'm sure he's Axel's, but we all share in the duties no matter which man fathered the children. They're *ours*, all together. "What do you say we get your daddies some refreshments?" I ask.

"Okay," he says, tugging me toward the refrigerator in the custom kitchen.

I waddle like the elephant I've become. I'm eight months pregnant, and I'm pretty sure this one will be a little girl at last. I had a dream two weeks ago, and Elder Amexaryl confirmed it.

Speaking of Elder Amexaryl, I've been apprenticing with her. Axel thinks I'm the perfect person to assume her role in the pack when she retires, though we don't know when that will be. No one knows her age and she won't tell, but when the time comes for her to rest and do what she feels like, I'll be ready. I'm pretty far along in my studies already. She says I'm a natural, being so submissive and in tune with the needs of others. She'll still attend the ceremonies, but they'll be conducted by me.

Everyone tromps into the kitchen and sits around the table. Aiden helps me hand out beers to the men and apple juice boxes to Coinin and Gavin. He hands me a non-alcoholic beer, since I can't drink much but developed a taste for beer when I first lived with the triplets.

Aidan helps Gavin into his high chair, then settles next to his brother and oversees him and his juice box.

I hand off the baby and lumber over to sit in Warrick's lap.

"How's my baby girl?" he says, smiling down at me.

"Happy as can be," I say, kissing him on the cheek and then snuggling into his big, strong chest. "Y'all have given me a dream life."

"As it should be," he says with a contented sigh.

The others beam at me from their places around the table.

"And how's this baby-girl?" Warrick asks, stroking my massive belly with his large hand.

The warmth is soothing, and I close my eyes for a moment. I've got everything a woman could want—a fantastic family, a beautiful home that we all fit in with room to grow, and a kick-ass community of welcoming wolves.

"Oh!" Warrick exclaims.

My eyes pop open.

Warrick's eyes widen and he grins. "She's saying hello to daddy number one."

"Hey, I'm daddy number one," Axel says, rising to step toward me.

"You're all daddy number one," Coinin says, rushing over.

Gavin sits in his high chair and sucks down his apple juice as six sets of hands pat my belly, feeling our new baby girl kick.

It's a good life. Hard-won, for sure, though. We've survived hurricanes, floods, assaults on our lives, hunting mishaps, heartbreak, break-ups, make-ups—with what Ethan calls all-night fuck-a-thons that make us too exhausted to hold a grudge—and so much more. But through it all, we have each other, and that's what matters. We have a beautiful home, a thriving family, and most of all, we have love, because that's what keeps us together in the end.

Return to the Pack

The End.

This concludes the *Rejected Mate* trilogy! Thank you for reading!

You can read many more of Alexa's books on Amazon, including these stories set in the same world as Luna's.

Academy of Sorcery (complete series: RH witches & wizards, kick-ass main character, high heat, action packed).
1. Term 1: Unleashing Trials
2. Term 2: Fallen Master
3. Term 3: Shadow Magic
4. Term 4: Secret Power

Feline Royals (complete series: RH taboo dark romance, shifters, high heat, fast burn).
1. Broken Princess
2. Captive Princess
3. Hunted Princess
4. Fallen Princess

Heartland Forest duet (complete duo, fae & werewolves).